JENNIFER S. ALDERSON

Death by Flamenco

An Easter Murder in Seville

To Jasper, my wonderful son and in-house environmentalist. Keep spreading the word, little man.

Contents

1

Jealous Rivals

April 6—Seattle, Washington

"Mercy," Dotty Thompson declared as she frowned at Lana's telephone screen. "That blog post is so cruel. It really does not sound like Chet. Maybe he was hacked."

"You know him?" Lana sank back into Dotty's couch as her boss's dogs bounced into the room, announcing their arrival with a bark. Rodney the pug pushed his head under Lana's hand while Chipper the Jack Russell terrier danced on her lap.

"I don't know why I am surprised. You do seem to know pretty much everyone of importance in the travel industry," Lana muttered as she petted both dogs.

Dotty was the owner of Wanderlust Tours, a company specializing in high-end tours to a plethora of European destinations. Dotty's company was quite successful, thanks as much to her many corporate connections, as her charm and business sense.

Lana's boss blushed. "Now, I don't know about that, but I do like to keep tabs on the major players in the travel industry. You know that saying—keep your friends close but your enemies closer."

Despite her boss's serious expression, Lana had to suppress a giggle. Since Lana began working for her more than a year ago, Dotty had become more of a friend and confidant than simply her employer. She knew for certain that the older lady had neither a mean bone in her body nor enemies.

Dotty handed Lana back her phone, then plopped down onto the couch next to her. Chipper and Rodney immediately shifted to their mistress's lap. Lana chuckled, knowing she couldn't compete with Dotty's doting.

"And in point of fact, I don't know Chet Rogers personally, though I have read all of his travel guides and I do follow his blog," Dotty continued while scratching her canines' backs. "But anyone working in the travel industry with sense in their head would read his posts. The Only Footprints travel guides really are the best ones available, which is why I give all of my employees a copy of them, as well."

Lana nodded, knowing that Dotty did her best to prepare her guides for their upcoming tours by presenting them with a stack of pamphlets, travel guides, and notes others had made during previous tours. This packet was extremely useful for the tours and also provided Lana with background information for the blog articles she wrote about the tourist attractions her groups visited.

Until she had read Chet's latest blog post, she had been looking forward to meeting him in person. There was an Only Footprints guidebook available for every country in Europe, and each was updated biannually. His lists of places to stay, eat, and visit were incredibly comprehensive. Lana often wondered whether there was any truth to the company's claim that Chet personally visited each and every place mentioned in his guidebooks. If that was so, Lana figured he was on the road even more than she was.

"But I follow lots of travel blogs, including yours," Dotty rushed to add. "Reading your *Travel Time* posts is a fun way for me to see what kinds of adventures you and your guests have had."

"Thanks, Dotty, for all the likes and positive comments. It is nice to know someone is reading my blog."

Dotty clicked her tongue. "Stop being so modest. Most of your posts already had hundreds of likes before I saw them. If your mother keeps helping you with the advertising, then I'm afraid I won't have a guide for much longer."

Lana's mother, the owner of a renowned advertising agency based out of Seattle, had been helping her monetize her *Travel Time* blog to the point that it was pulling in a small income every month. As proud as she was that her blog was in the black, it was nowhere near enough to replace her current salary.

Lana started to pooh-pooh Dotty's comment about her quitting Wanderlust Tours to blog full time, when she noticed tears forming in the older woman's eyes. She grabbed her boss's hands and squeezed them tight.

"Don't worry, I can't quit. If I do, I won't have anything to write about!" she teased, getting a smile out of Dotty. Lana truly couldn't imagine resigning anytime soon. Working as a guide for Wanderlust Tours had to be the best job she'd ever had—well, besides being an investigative journalist. But that door was well and truly closed.

These days, writing her *Travel Time* blog posts was her creative outlet. It was fun to see the number of likes and shares increase, the longer she worked at it. A few of her posts had even been shared on a popular travel website's social media account, which led to her being discovered by the organizers of the travel conference in Seville, Spain, that she and her tour group were about to visit. At least, that was how Dotty had said the organizers had found her. Lana was still in shock that she had been asked to sit on the same panel as the other six professional travel writers, publishers, and bloggers—all of whom she admired deeply. And it was perfect to combine with her tour of Andalucía—taking place during Easter week, no less!

Unfortunately, her participation on the panel was also the reason why Chet Rogers had tried to smear her name, along with the other five panelists', in his latest blog post. Reading his article had tempered her excitement about the upcoming trip. In a few days, she would be sitting on the same stage as Chet. If he dared to make a fool of her in the media, how would he act towards her in person?

As much as Lana wanted to take part in this panel discussion, she had no interest in being somebody's punching bag.

"But what am I going to do about Chet Rogers?" Lana asked, bringing her boss's attention back to the matter at hand. Lana was scheduled to leave for

Seville tomorrow morning, and she needed to figure out her strategy before boarding that plane.

When Dotty began fretting instead of answering, Lana added, "He seems to dislike everyone on the panel. He even insulted Becky and Nick Soho, claiming that video subscription channels such as theirs are undermining the future of the travel writing industry. Can you believe it? The Sohos have been voted the world's most popular travel bloggers for three years running! What on earth did those two do to deserve his wrath?"

Dotty clicked her tongue. "No good comes from bad-mouthing another. It is too bad Chet felt the need to post this, but I suspect he was trying to put you all in your place before the conference starts. The panel discussion is on the future of travel writing, and as far as I know, Chet's focus is still on print. I bet he feels threatened by the rest of you."

"He is being honored with a lifetime achievement award!" Lana exclaimed. "You would think he would not have to worry about the competition anymore."

Dotty pursed her lips. "I suppose that is one way of looking at it. He has been writing guidebooks for thirty years, so he knows all the ins and outs of the business. But if you take a good look at the suggestions in his most recent guides, you will notice that they cater primarily to the high-end crowd. Which, let's face it, is a smaller, older audience. They provide precious few recommendations for younger people looking for more adventurous things to do. Travel has become so much more accessible in the past few years, with all those cheap airline tickets and Airbnb-style accommodations popping up around the globe like mushrooms. It is as if Chet doesn't recognize that the art of travel has changed in the past thirty years. I can imagine that he is feeling a little behind, in comparison to the bloggers he is sitting on the panel with. Mind you, I'm not saying he was right to print those offensive things about you all, but it sure seems like he wants to prove that his guidebooks are still relevant."

Lana stared at her phone, reviewing the many negative comments and accusations filling the screen. "You might be right. But I do wonder what the others think of this article."

"Probably the same as you."

"Maybe I should back out of the conference."

"Don't be silly," Dotty snapped and sat up so fast that her dogs sprung off her lap and ran under the dining room table. "I'm sorry for scaring you, boys," she called out to her pets before whipping around to face Lana. "You can't bow out. These kinds of chances rarely come along, especially when you are just starting out. If you cancel now, I can guarantee you that no other conference will ever ask you to participate. Besides, I cannot imagine any of the others are considering backing out of the panel discussion because of Chet's offensive article."

"But Chet may further destroy my reputation if I do go! He accused me of being a worthless nobody that has no right sitting on the panel in the first place," Lana said, then held up her phone, reading part of Chet's article. "'Lana Hansen's presence on the panel says quite a bit about the diminishing quality of this once prestigious trade show. All I can think is that Ms. Hansen must know one of the organizers and called in a personal favor.'"

Lana looked back up at her boss, who was blushing red, and asked, "Do you really expect me to sit next to that vile man and not say anything about his article or cruel comments? What if he attacks me during the discussion? What am I supposed to do—sit there and take it? Or come back with a strong retort? I don't have a good comeback yet, at least not one I could repeat on television."

"Honey, there is strength in numbers. There are five other people who want his head on a stick, all sitting right next to you. And if you think about it, him bad-mouthing the entire panel has only weakened his own credibility. You were all chosen because you are the best at what you do—or the most promising," Dotty said with a nod towards Lana. "It's an international conference being attended by thousands of travel professionals, and your panel discussion is going to be covered by the world's press, as well as livestreamed on the internet! Try to put his words out of your mind and focus on all the good it will do your business."

Lana nodded, knowing Dotty was right on all counts. It was good to remember that she wouldn't be the only one worried about a confrontation with Chet. Because the other panel participants were on her tour, she would have a chance to talk to them about that awful article before they met with Chet. She was charming enough to get them all on her side before the conference began. At least, she hoped that she was.

Dotty tapped the couch, and her dogs tore back into the room, yapping as they ran onto their mistress's lap. "You know, sweetness might just be the best revenge."

Lana cocked an eyebrow at her.

"What if you introduce yourself to Chet as if you had not read the article? Hopefully he will be so embarrassed by his words and actions that he will do the same. He does have to sit in the same room with you all for three hours."

Dotty had a heart of gold and seemed unable to accept that people could be truly rotten to the core. Lana wished she had Dotty's sense of grace, but she did not.

"Are you serious—after he called me a nobody? I mean, my blog may not be as popular as any of the other panelists', but I made the cut so I must have done something right to get the organizers' attention."

"That's right." Dotty nodded encouragingly. "Which means you can afford to be the better person in this situation."

"I suppose…" The mere idea of being kind and courteous to Chet made her stomach turn. Yet dealing with him wouldn't be that much different than dealing with an irate client. Luckily, that didn't happen very often, but occasionally she did get a tour participant who was impossible to please. Perhaps pretending he was simply an irritating client would do the trick.

When Lana's frown deepened, instead of diminishing, Dotty added, "Besides, nobody reads his blog anymore."

"Good try," Lana chuckled. Though she appreciated Dotty's attempts at minimizing her concerns, Lana knew she was lying. Only Footprints guidebooks were one of the best-read and bestselling travel series in the world. Even if his blog didn't garner as much attention as his books did, Lana assumed it would still be read by many.

Dotty scooted her dogs gently off her lap and jumped up. "It's tea time. Fresh mint?"

Lana nodded, letting her boss's words sink in, when her phone rang. It was her old friend, Jeremy.

"Hey, Lana. My news desk is going crazy about this new blog post written by Chet Rogers, the publisher of Only Footprints guidebooks. He sent a press release about his upcoming appearance at that travel conference next week and included a link to his blog. His latest article has gone viral online. When I saw you were involved, I offered to call, instead of one of my reporters. Would you mind giving me a comment or response that we can use in our article?"

"Oh, no," Lana mumbled. Jeremy was not only a good friend, he was also the editor of a regional newspaper. Chet Rogers, being from Seattle originally, was a local legend in the Pacific Northwest. She should have known that the regional press would be interested in covering his lifetime achievement award. *That explains the timing of the article*, Lana thought. He must have published it when he did to ensure it was also covered by the local media.

She covered the receiver with her hand and yelled to Dotty, "Chet's blog post has gone viral, and Jeremy wants a response for his newspaper."

Dotty rushed back from the kitchen, sprigs of fresh mint in her hand. "Goodness, that was fast. You have no comment at this time, not even for Jeremy. But if his team is writing about it, you better believe other news media are, too. You might want to turn off your ringer."

Lana sighed and nodded. "That sounds like good advice. Let me deal with Jeremy." She started to turn away when she nodded at the mint in Dotty's hands. "I think we are going to need something stronger than tea in a minute."

"You're right. I'll make us mojitos. No sense wasting the mint."

Lana's forehead creased. Her boss was no teetotaler, but Dotty usually stuck with white wine or spritzers. "When did you learn to make a mojito?"

"Earl loves cocktails so I've been taking mixology classes."

"That's neat. I didn't know amateurs could take those classes, too."

"Earl says my Bloody Marys are the best he's ever tasted." Dotty turned towards the staircase, as if to make certain her boyfriend hadn't entered the room, before whispering, "My secret is an extra splash of Worcestershire sauce."

"I won't tell Earl," Lana said with a wink. Her boss was full of surprises.

2

Social Media Heroes

April 8—Day One of the World Travelers Expo in Seville, Spain

Lana bounced on her heels like a nervous schoolgirl as she waited for the elevator door to open and take her down to the lobby and her awaiting clients. Instead of the usual mix of wealthy Seattleites, her current tour group was a who's who of popular travel writers, bloggers, and publishers. In addition to being a major sponsor of the prestigious World Travelers Expo, Dotty had also gifted a weeklong tour of Andalucía to a group of social influencers in the hope they would praise Wanderlust Tours in their social media and publications.

Because they were flying in from all over the world, her group was to meet up in the hotel's restaurant a few minutes before the travel expo's kickoff dinner was scheduled to begin. After she had crossed the vast lobby, Lana pushed away a wave of nervousness before opening the restaurant door. In the corner were most of her guests, already sitting around a large table.

Her heart skipped a beat when Becky Soho, the creator of her favorite travel videos, rose and smiled at her. "Well, if it isn't Lana Hansen. I am an admirer of your blog." Her short bob jiggled as she moved, framing her heart-shaped face perfectly.

Lana's mouth fell open. Becky Soho had read her blog! *I could die happy now,* she thought. Becky and her husband, Nick, were the creative geniuses

"

behind the *Life's A Journey* blog and YouTube subscription channel. Lana just loved reading their funny stories and watching their interesting videos about their adventures to off-the-beaten-path destinations that were often overlooked by mainstream travel guides. She wasn't the only one; the couple had been voted the world's best travel bloggers by the Travelers Channel and *Adventure!* magazine three years running. Their popularity meant that their video feeds were laden with advertising. Lana didn't mind; it was worth sitting through a few short ads to see where the daring duo were off to next.

Though Lana didn't know where the American couple were currently based out of, she did know that they had flown in from Goa, India, last night. She blushed as she muttered her thanks. "I can say the same."

Nick Soho, a ruggedly attractive man in his early forties, rose and offered Lana a hand. Both were deeply tanned; Becky's brown hair was tinged with blond highlights, and Nick's was so bleached out—from the sun, Lana assumed—that it was almost white. His pearly grin stole her breath away.

"Nick Soho. Good to meet you, Lana."

Even his voice is sexy, she thought, enjoying its deep timbre. "You, too, Nick. I am a huge fan."

They seemed so down to earth in their videos and appeared to be in real life, too. She was impressed; apparently their enormous success had not gone to their heads.

"Your recent videos of Madagascar are incredible!" Lana gushed. "They really make me want to visit the island. You're both so natural in front of the camera that I bet it won't be long before a television channel picks you up."

Becky shone in delight, then leaned over and whispered, "You are right about that. But until the official announcement, my lips are sealed." She mimed locking her mouth and throwing away an invisible key before breaking out into a loud guffaw.

Even her laugh is endearing, Lana thought, feeling like a silly fan girl.

Hoping to maintain a sense of authority, she turned to the rest of the table and waved. "Hello, everyone! It is a pleasure to meet you all in person. I am Lana Hansen. Randy Wright and I can't wait to explore Andalucía with you after the conference."

Where is Randy? she wondered as she held up the sheets of paper in her hand. "I know that our tour doesn't technically begin until after the conference has concluded, but I do have a copy of the latest itinerary for you all—"

"That's a shame. What a waste of paper. Couldn't you have emailed it to us?" a younger woman asked as she frowned at Lana.

She recognized the speaker as environmental and sustainability blogger Amber Laurent, well-known for her *Lessen Your Carbon Footprint* blog. Originally from France, Amber was now based out of Saint-Martin, an island in the Caribbean Sea. Amber's red hair was twisted into two loose braids that hung over her shoulders, each with several curly hairs escaping. Her skin was as white as porcelain, and she looked even younger than her twenty-three years. The extra-large bottle of suntan lotion and floppy hat on the table in front of her might have been the key to maintaining her youthful appearance, Lana realized. She was dressed in a loose, ankle-length dress made from a flowery pattern printed on what appeared to be a rough cotton.

Is it hemp? Lana wondered before stammering, "Gosh, I'm sorry. You are right. I didn't even think about the environmental impact—"

"Some would argue that the excessive use of email and internet-based apps wastes far more energy and is doing more damage to our environment, than printing on paper," a young man sitting at the back of the group piped up. The lankiness of his body was accentuated by his brightly colored Bermuda shorts and loose-fitting Hawaiian T-shirt.

"Our reliance on computers is fueling a massive overreliance on electricity that most countries cannot satisfy," he reasoned. "The problem will only worsen as more electric cars replace gas- and diesel-powered ones."

Amber's self-righteous expression transformed quickly into a mask of irritation as she whipped around to face him. Before she could retort, Lana turned and smiled at the young man. "Are you Dwight Anderson?"

He half rose from his chair. "At your service."

"You are a writer for that eMagazine—*Travel Wise*, correct?" Lana asked. Dwight was not speaking on the panel, but had been scheduled to give a workshop titled "Exploring the Dark Side of the Travel Industry," which was why Dotty had offered him a spot on this tour. However, his workshop had been canceled at the last minute due to a lack of interest. Dotty didn't have the heart to cancel his trip as well, which was why he was along for the ride. As far as Lana knew, he was still planning on attending the travel conference.

Dwight's face lit up. "That's right. It's my magazine—I'm the editor and write most of the articles. Have you read much of my work?"

Lana's grin faltered. "Your last two issues. You make some interesting arguments in your essays."

She had made a point of reading his work when she saw he was on the tour, but she was less than impressed with his digital magazine. His suggestions for places to visit were exactly the sort of tourist traps one would find listed in general travel blogs and guides. Lana vastly preferred learning about places that were truly off the beaten path.

But what really bothered her about Dwight's magazine was the underlying tone of self-righteousness he used when describing a place. He seemed more interested in passing moral judgment on the city and the tourists who visited it, instead of actually describing the location. His recent article about Amsterdam was nothing more than a long rant about tourists who only go there to visit the prostitutes in the Red Light District and smoke themselves silly. By reading his essay, she had no sense of visiting the city and wondered whether he had actually ever been to the Netherlands.

Dwight regarded her critically, giving Lana the feeling that her opinion meant nothing to him, before finally asking, "You write that *Travel Time* blog, correct?"

"Yes, I do."

"I checked you out after I saw you had been added to the panel. Your blog posts are quite quaint; I'm certain visitors preferring photos over text would enjoy it. But you really haven't been doing this long. Because you are speaking on the most important panel discussion of the expo, I would have expected you to have posted more often. It's a missed opportunity on the part of the organizers—they could have asked me to fill in."

"Thanks," Lana said, the look on her face hopefully making clear that she was being sarcastic. *Why does Dwight think he is so superior?* she wondered. She didn't post to her blog more than twice a month these days, but her photo-rich articles were well shared and highly ranked in several important search engines—owing much in part to her mother's help with the advertising. Yet Dwight's comment only reinforced her own seeds of self-doubt. Why did the organization ask her to fill in, instead of someone with more experience and followers? Lana made a mental note to ask her boss the next time they spoke.

The gorgeous young woman sitting next to Dwight held out a manicured hand to Lana. "Serena Tan—lovely to meet you," she purred.

The Singaporean beauty's high cheekbones and full red lips made her impossible to ignore. She was dressed in spandex leggings that left nothing to the imagination, and her long, black hair was pulled back into a loose ponytail, revealing hoop earrings. A crop top enhanced her ample bosom and exposed the young woman's jewel-encrusted navel ring. Another glittery symbol in the shape of a footprint adorned her chest.

Serena's makeup was also catwalk ready, which made sense considering she was a lifestyle blogger with millions of followers. Lana wondered how early Serena rose each day, knowing it would have taken her all morning to re-create the young lady's extensive makeup.

Lana looked closely at the tiny footprint on Serena's chest, knowing it was the source of contention between the young blogger and Chet Rogers. In his blog post, he accused Serena of copying his logo in an attempt to use his popularity to sell her new clothing line. Considering how many followers she had, Lana doubted that Serena would have intentionally done so. The young woman was just twenty-two years old and already one of the world's most popular lifestyle bloggers.

Lana gently took Serena's hand, almost afraid to squeeze too hard for fear of breaking it. It felt limp to the touch. "The pleasure is all mine. Your blog is quite incredible."

Serena's eyebrows rose slightly as she looked Lana up and down.

Lana cringed, realizing how boring her travel-casual wardrobe—loose-fitting slacks, a tunic-style blouse, and leather sandals—would be to the fashion-conscious blogger.

"It's nice to meet a follower," Serena responded politely.

Lana couldn't help blushing as she realized how insignificant her own blog was in comparison to Serena's. Of course the young blogger wouldn't see her as an equal simply because she also had a travel blog. Lana would have to seriously increase her number of followers to be in the same league as Serena.

She looked to the three empty seats, wondering where her fellow guide, Randy Wright, and the last two guests were. As she pulled out her phone to call him, Randy burst through the door, looking slightly out of breath.

"Hello, everyone! I found a few stragglers in the lobby." He stepped back to allow a distinguished-looking couple to pass.

The man was in his sixties, yet the woman on his arm was significantly younger. The way he laid his hand on her backside told Lana that it was not his daughter.

Whereas the older man seemed at home in his stylish ensemble of tailored slacks, white dress shirt, and camel-colored jacket, his partner seemed a bit nervous in her expensive-looking sundress.

"Hello, everyone. I'm Ted Castle, and this is my fiancée, Erica," he announced. "Please do thank Dotty for inviting us along."

Lana nodded, knowing that her boss had been a good friend of Ted's first wife. When his wife had been diagnosed with a rare blood disorder and needed experimental treatment two years earlier, Dotty had chipped in. Unfortunately, the medicines didn't help, and Ted's wife soon slipped into a coma that she would never come out of. Lana recalled Dotty saying that when the doctors suggested pulling the plug, Ted had his wife brought home. It cost him a fortune to care for her, but he wanted to do all he could to make her last days as comfortable as possible. Dotty had confided that Ted had to use up all his savings and took out loans against his business, as well, to pay for everything.

Dotty had also mentioned that Ted and Chet had started Only Footprints together, but after his wife became so ill, they'd had a falling-out, and Ted had left the company. Apparently her boss had not been privy to the details because the horrid comments Chet made about Ted's lack of financial sense and how the company had flourished since his departure were cruel surprises.

"I apologize if we have held up the taxi," Ted stated, though his tone gave away no hint of remorse as he and his fiancée slipped into the empty seats.

"Not at all," Lana enthused, knowing how much Dotty wanted him, in particular, to have a wonderful week. "In fact, you two are just in time. The taxi should be arriving any minute."

"Hey, Ted." Dwight leaned over the other guests to make eye contact with the older man. "I am surprised to see you here. After all that crap Chet wrote about you, I didn't think you would want to sit on the same panel with him."

"You'd do better not to mention that name to me again," Ted growled. "Besides, why would I want to stay away? I doubt Chet will actually show his face at the conference, not after all the negative reactions to his latest blog post. And even if that weasel does, what is a better revenge than confronting him with his lies in front of millions of viewers?"

Lana's eyebrows shot up. It was clear from Chet's latest blog post that the two business partners had not parted ways as friends, but the insinuations Chet made about Ted's inept actions while serving as Only Footprints' chief officer of finance were vague at best. She made a mental note to look into the two men's past later.

"You have got a point there," Dwight murmured. "Chet knows I'll strangle him with my bare hands if he does."

Lana recalled that Chet had written that Dwight's inability to convey a sense of place in his writing led him to describe everything with the eye of a dissatisfied traveler, one incapable of enjoying the experiences around him.

As harsh as Chet's comments were, in this case, she did agree with him. There was little joy or sense of wonder in Dwight's articles, which for Lana were the reasons why she loved to travel most. There was something magical about seeing so much of Europe and experiencing all the different cultures present within it.

"What are we going to do about Chet?" Becky asked tentatively. "That article was defamation in my book, but our lawyer says it will be near impossible to prove." She looked to her husband, who nodded in agreement.

"We need to confront him together during the panel discussion—if he actually comes to the conference," Amber implored.

"I heard he is terminally ill and not even planning on being here. That is why he published that vile article," Serena said in a loud whisper, as if she was telling everyone a secret only she was privy to.

Dwight looked puzzled. "Really? I heard he had a new television show all lined up that was going to begin shooting in Europe next month."

"You shouldn't believe everything you read," Becky said. When she glanced at her husband, both began to snigger.

"What's so funny?" Dwight asked, his tone guarded.

"Nothing, sorry. I was trying to imagine Chet in front of a camera. The man is as stiff as a plank," Becky giggled.

"Well, I heard…" Her guests began talking over each other as they shared the latest online gossip, though it was pretty clear to Lana that no one really knew what Chet Rogers was up to or why he had written that horrible article.

"Has anyone seen him walking around the hotel or know if he's checked in yet? Everyone attending the conference is staying here, and he is being honored at the dinner tonight. If he isn't present for that, I bet he won't attend the panel discussion," Nick said.

A voice of reason, Lana thought as Dwight added, "You're right. We'll know soon enough if Chet had the guts to show."

3

Lifetime of Achievements

Lana's foot tapped in rhythm with the Spanish guitarist, his fingers flying over his instrument's strings as two dancers twirled and strutted around the small podium. The flamenco dancers, singer, and musician were engaged in a centuries-old expression of passion, love, and longing that was magical to see performed live.

The male dancer was clad in a tight-fitting black suit, and his female counterpart had on a red and black polka dot dress with a lacy shawl over her shoulders and a large comb in her hair. Lana was mesmerized by the dancers' highly stylized movements. The singer's voice was infused with a haunting melancholy that spoke to her soul. His words seemed to swim through the guitar's driving melody that was perfectly timed to the dancers' steps and sways.

Lana couldn't wait to try dancing like that during the flamenco workshop scheduled for the last night of the conference. She studied the female dancer's dress and posture, wondering whether she would be able to fit into the tight bodice or get her hands to form the same dramatic gestures.

She was surprised to see that the dancers did not hold hands, but danced alongside each other as they executed choreographed steps in which they seemed to circle each other. Their bodies passed close by each other without actually touching, yet they kept their eyes locked on each other as they danced. Despite the fact that they did not embrace, it was quite a sensual performance.

When the ensemble stopped and took their bows, the two-thousand-strong audience broke out into a tremendous applause. As soon as they had left the stage, the house lights went back on, and teams of waiters bearing large platters of food began weaving through the tables.

After their waiters filled their table with a plethora of tiny bowls and saucer-sized plates, Lana was initially concerned it wouldn't be enough for her group. Yet, after sampling the meats and vegetables dripping in oils and rich marinades, she realized the portions were small for a reason.

At first, Amber had been quite vocal in her disapproval of the predominance of meat-based dishes and the effects of the beef industry on the planet, until Serena shoved a piece of marinated eggplant into her mouth. Lana had to hide a smile with the back of her hand when Amber's cries of protest turned to murmurs of happiness as she greedily sampled the grilled vegetables, baked cheeses, and roasted garlic.

Everyone seemed to be enjoying their meal, except Dwight. During dinner, Lana noticed him glaring at Ted whenever he thought the older man wasn't looking at him.

Ted must have noticed it, too. "Have we met before?" he asked while studying the young man's face.

Dwight's cheeks colored crimson. "You could say that. I applied as a writer for your new website, but you turned me down. I wondered why."

Ted laughed and slapped him on the back. "Don't take it personally. We received hundreds of applications for only a handful of freelance positions. You can always try again in a few months."

"Your rejection letter made it pretty clear that my work wasn't fit for your magazine."

"What is your name again, son?"

"Dwight Anderson."

Ted's face darkened briefly before an air of neutral professionalism settled on his face. "I do recall reading your work. I'm afraid your style really does not mesh with our vision."

"What do you want to feature on your website—photos of half-naked women playing in the waves and videos about where to find the best margarita?"

"That is a rather crass way of formulating it. We are planning on featuring short, flashy items about travel, with a focus on new trends and blogs to follow. You can always sign your eMagazine up for our digital subscription service, but I cannot guarantee that any of your articles will be read."

"Your new idea sounds perfect for so-called social influencers such as Serena and Amber, but don't your readers want to dig deeper into the travel experience?"

Both Serena and Amber glared at Dwight, who was apparently oblivious to the rudeness of his remark.

Ted did notice and looked to both women as he took business cards out of his jacket pocket. "It would be an honor to work with either one of you," he said as he handed both women one, before turning back to Dwight.

Ted's smile had vanished. "Since you feel the need to be so blunt, let me return the favor. We see travel as a wondrous experience, a chance to discover more about your true self while learning about other cultures and ways of life. Your style of writing is the antithesis of what we want to feature on our website."

Ted's voice remained calm, but his eyes had narrowed to slits.

His fiancée noticed and put her hand over his. "Aren't those decorations adorable? I bet those flag streamers would make a great shot for Instagram." Erica pulled an expensive-looking digital camera out of her enormous purse and handed it to Ted. "Why don't you take a few? You've got a far better eye than I do."

He kissed her on the forehead and rose to get closer to the streamers she had pointed out.

Dwight glowered at him for a moment, then turned to Serena and Amber. "What is it that you two have, that I do not?"

"Charisma and a passion for life?" Serena offered.

"A positive attitude and an appreciation of nature," Amber added.

Lana had to suppress a snort. So far, Amber was the opposite of positive. It was so strange to see how different her bubbly online persona was from the reality.

On her blog, Amber shared a plethora of tips as to how individuals could lessen their carbon footprint and improve their local environment. What could be a depressing topic, Amber managed to turn into a cheerful and uplifting one. Was her cranky attitude simply due to jet lag? Or was there something else that was making her tense?

Serena and Amber ignored Dwight and turned towards the stage just as the lights dimmed and the master of ceremonies stepped into the spotlight. Ted hurried back to the table and handed his fiancée the camera.

"Greetings, fellow travel lovers. How was your meal?" The MC cupped his hand to his ear as the crowd began yelling adjectives describing the delicious food. He chuckled into the microphone. "Glad to hear it. Before I ask the next musical performance to join me on stage, we want to honor one of the longest-working travel writers still active in the industry today. Please help me welcome to the stage Chet Rogers, writer and publisher of the legendary Only Footprints guidebooks."

The MC's eyes scanned the crowd until he spotted Chet rising from his table and waving enthusiastically to the crowd.

Lana recognized Chet from his signature wardrobe—a three-piece suit and bowtie. His appearance made him appear to be a gentlemanly tourist of a bygone era. She could imagine that his look worked well with the older, well-heeled crowd his guidebooks seemed to be written for.

Considering he was seated at the table in front of the stage, Lana figured it would take Chet mere seconds to reach the microphone. But he managed to extend the applause by walking around several tables, shaking hands as he went, before finally ascending the podium and grabbing a microphone.

"It is an honor to be here with you tonight," Chet enthused as the MC clapped along with the audience, welcoming him to the stage.

Chet's voice had a high-pitched, nasal tone that she had not expected. It seemed to fit a young girl, not a man in his mid-sixties.

"We could not help but notice that you are celebrating thirty years in the business—quite a feat, really! We all look forward to hearing you speak during the panel discussion on our last day—which sold out in record time, by the way." The MC grinned at the audience. "Which is why we will be livestreaming the discussion in the main expo hall so everyone can hear it."

After the next round of applause died down, the MC asked, "We want to give our audience a chance to learn more about you and your publications. What is your secret to success—how has Only Footprints remained one of the bestselling series of travel guides for so long?"

"My high standards. I wrote all of the original guides thirty years ago by hand." He held up his right hand and chuckled as he looked to his audience. "Can you believe it?"

His attempt at a joke got a polite giggle from the crowd.

"I pride myself on visiting all of the places listed in my books, which does not happen with all of my competitors, let me assure you. My motto is, if you haven't been there, you shouldn't write about it."

Dwight's guffaw echoed through the hallway, causing Chet to glare into the public before adding, "It will be near impossible to find a qualified writer to take my place once I am gone."

The MC suddenly looked stricken and laid a hand on Chet's arm. "You are not planning on retiring anytime soon, are you? Or can we trust that Only Footprints guidebooks will live on a while longer?"

"I'm not going anywhere," he resounded into the microphone. "I suspect I'll be one of those people who ends up keeling over while I'm on the road."

"Many years from now, we hope," the MC said.

"Until that day comes, you can expect the same high quality from Only Footprints."

"That is wonderful news—right, everyone?" The MC looked to the audience, and they began clapping again. When it subsided, he added, "A little birdie tells me that you have a new project in the works."

Chet glowed. "That's right."

"You have been a traditional, print-based publisher for more than thirty years, and now you are about to make a splash in the digital world. I understand you are about to launch a new website that will revolutionize how we view and share travel-related digital content?"

"You are correct. It will be a pay-per-read system. Through our platform, readers will have access to any travel article published digitally in the past ten years. There will be no more need for readers to subscribe to several magazines to stay up to date. They can peruse all of their content and only pay to read what interests them most. Several of the world's most important print magazines have already expressed interest in adding their articles to my service."

A strange gurgling noise made Lana look away from Chet and towards the sound's source. Ted was bent over the table, a napkin over his mouth, as his body quivered. His fiancée was apparently also concerned because she began slapping him hard on the back.

After Ted's coughing subsided, Lana rose and squatted between the engaged couple. "Are you okay?"

"Yes," he whispered back. "I just swallowed my drink wrong, that's all."

"I about choked, too, when Chet mentioned his new website. That sounds so similar to what you are doing," his fiancée said.

Ted began coughing again.

"Do you need the Heimlich?" Erica asked, her voice laced with concern.

Ted waved her off. "No," he sputtered, "but I could use some fresh air."

As they rose to walk towards the exit, Lana heard Ted say to Erica, "I need to call my lawyer."

"What was that all about?" Randy asked, one eye on his departing guests.

"Nothing, Ted just needs some fresh air," Lana explained. Chet was still fielding the MC's questions about his new website's subscription service, which—based on the resounding applause—was well received by this audience.

As the last of the claps faded out, the MC said, "Before we ask our musical guests to join us onstage, we have a special award for Chet."

A scantily clad woman came onto the stage, carrying a large, gold-plated trophy shaped like a globe. On the pedestal, "Celebrating thirty years of Only Footprints guidebooks" was inscribed.

"It is our deep honor to present you with World Travelers Expo's very first Lifetime Achievement Award. May Only Footprints enjoy another thirty years of success!" the MC exclaimed as the young woman handed Chet his trophy.

He held it up high, and most audience members stood up to cheer him on.

Between the claps, Lana noticed her own guests were far from pleased.

"That man is a dinosaur," Amber said to Serena.

"Yeah, he should be extinct," Serena replied.

"Cheers to that idea," Dwight added.

Becky and Nick locked eyes yet said nothing as they slowly clapped.

4

Midnight Caller

It took a lot of cajoling to get her group into their taxi after the travel expo's first event had officially ended. Lots of great tapas, fun entertainment, and an endless supply of sangria made it a memorable night.

After they'd made certain everyone had gotten back to their rooms, Lana said goodnight to Randy, then made her way slowly to hers. She hadn't had that much to drink—they had a busy day tomorrow and she didn't want to be hungover—but she was exhausted, nonetheless.

Her eyes were having trouble focusing when she reached her door. Her fingers locked onto the slip of plastic deep inside her purse, but the key card didn't work. Only when she examined it more closely did she notice the credit card logo.

Cursing her tiredness, she opened up her purse again and was scrounging around for the correct card when Chet strode down the hallway, preening like a peacock. He whipped out his key card and opened his door without trouble, sneering at Lana the entire time.

"Oh great, he's my neighbor," she mumbled as her hand wrapped around the correct card. After she closed the door to her room, she lay against it, already dreaming about the bath she was too tired to actually take, when a sharp knock made her turn and look through the peephole. It wasn't Chet knocking on her door, was it?

Lana didn't see anyone on her threshold, but did see Serena standing in front of Chet's now opening door. *What the heck is going on?* she wondered and pushed her eye closer to the glass.

"Well, well—look who's here. Come in, my dear," Lana heard Chet say before Serena entered his room.

When he leaned out into the hallway and put the "Do Not Disturb" sign on the door handle, his lecherous grin turned Lana's stomach.

"Gross," she muttered. Were they having an affair? Lana could not imagine such a lovely young woman would choose to be with such a vulgar old man. Was Chet blackmailing Serena somehow? And if so, for what exactly? The more Lana thought about the reasons for Serena and Chet's midnight rendezvous, the more disgusted she became.

5

The Truth Will Come Out

April 9—Day Two of the World Travelers Expo in Seville, Spain

When Lana arose the next morning, she still had that image of Chet's leering grin in her mind. Was Serena still in his room? Before she could finish dressing, a sharp knock drew her back to her door's peephole.

She was in time to see Dwight force his way through Chet's open door, then slam it shut. Angry words ensued, their content muffled by the thick wood. Were Serena and Dwight somehow romantically involved and the younger man was there to defend her honor? Or was Dwight's beef with Chet unrelated to his love life?

Lana finished dressing in record time and ran into the hallway just as Chet's door burst open again.

"At least do what you promised. You owe me that much," Dwight yelled as he backed out into the hallway.

"Over my dead body. I don't owe you anything. Now get out," Chet raged as he pushed Dwight hard, sending the young man stumbling backwards, before he slammed his door shut.

As Dwight fell onto his backside, he screamed, "The truth will come out—whether you like it or not!"

He sprung up and pounded on the wooden door so hard that Lana was worried it might shatter. She rushed down the hallway, hoping to be able to defuse the situation. However, one look at Dwight's face—a mask of pure rage—and she wished that she had called Randy first. Luckily for her, he had apparently already heard the scuffle and was hustling down the hallway towards them.

"What's going on?" Randy called out when he caught sight of Lana. Dwight was still pounding on the door, apparently unaware that almost all of the guests along the long hallway were peeking their heads out of their doors, watching the unfolding scene.

"I'm not sure," Lana said. She held her hands out in front of her as if they might be able to deflect her client's anger. "Dwight? What happened?"

Dwight pulled back from Chet's door and glared at both tour guides, now only a few feet away. "It's none of your business," he said, before sprinting down the hall.

Both guides watched him go. "Chet really does get under people's skin, doesn't he?" Randy asked.

"Sure looks like it. We better keep an eye on Dwight today. The last thing we need is for him to attack Chet and be arrested," Lana replied.

Randy nodded, but his mouth formed a grimace. "That's going to be a challenge, seeing as we are spending the day at the travel expo. The main hall alone is the size of four football fields, and Dwight isn't exactly a chatty guy. I don't see him wanting me to tag along all day."

Lana sucked in her breath, knowing he was right. "I guess all we can do is try. At least we know from experience that Dotty seems to have access to great lawyers in pretty much every European country."

Randy laid a hand on her shoulder. "Let's hope that if we do need one, it's only for a minor incident, and not another death."

"Hear, hear," Lana said through gritted teeth.

6

Keeping A Promise

When Lana entered the breakfast hall a few minutes later, she was surprised to see Dwight already seated with a plate full of food in front of him.

She approached him slowly, asking softly, "Are you okay?"

"Of course. I slept like a baby. Thanks for asking," Dwight said loudly then bit into a slice of cured ham.

Lana looked at him, wondering why he was pretending everything was alright, when she realized he must be embarrassed by this morning's events. Considering all of her guests were staying on the same floor, she had to assume most of the tour group had heard Dwight and Chet arguing.

She and Randy ensured the rest of their guests were sated before scooping up their own first meal of the day. Lana took in the extensive buffet, glad she hadn't drunk so much that she felt hungover. It would have been a shame to have to pass over the scrumptious *churro relleno con chocolate*—a hot dog-shaped pastry filled with warm chocolate. It melted so quickly in her mouth that she had even gone back for seconds.

Becky and Nick were checking their social media between bites. Serena and Amber were comparing Instagram accounts. Based on their body language, Lana sensed a strong mutual respect between the two social media influencers. Dwight sat across from the two young women, seemingly content to listen to their conversation.

Lana had been surprised to see the two women hitting it off so well, until she realized that, despite being very different kinds of bloggers, both women were in their twenties and very much in touch with their generation's ideals. In addition, both had an astronomical number of social media followers and had recently launched lines of travel-related products. Lana had trouble fathoming that millions of people were eager to hear what these two young women had to say, but then she was more than twenty years older than either one.

Ted sat at a separate table so he could better prepare for his presentation about his new website. All Lana could gather from the brief description in the travel expo's brochure was that it included a pay-per-read service, similar to Chet's project. She was looking forward to learning more about it during Ted's presentation later today.

His fiancée was not holding a gadget, but instead fidgeted with the sleeves of her designer blouse. Lana felt sorry for the woman, who was clearly not in her element. *How did those two meet?* she wondered.

Before she could engage Erica in conversation, Randy leaned over and asked, "Do you know what time the taxi is supposed to arrive?"

She glanced at her watch. "Any minute. I'll check outside to see if it is already here."

"Great, I'll get the group out to the lobby," Randy said.

As they rose, Chet Rogers swept by.

"Someone should put that liar in his place," Dwight said quite loudly, clearly hoping Chet would hear him. If he did, Chet showed no sign of it and instead kept striding along at the same pace towards the exit.

The lobby doors were propped open to accommodate the stream of conference visitors leaving to catch their shuttle buses to the expo center. Lana hustled outside to see whether their taxi was waiting for them. Though she didn't see their cab, she did see Chet waiting next to the open doors while his taxi maneuvered closer to the curbside.

Recalling her promise to Dotty, Lana strode over to him. She figured it would be better to get this over with now than to introduce herself right before the panel discussion was about to begin. Lana had a feeling this wasn't going to be a light and friendly chat, as Dotty had hoped it would be.

When she approached, Lana said loudly, "Chet Rogers. It is an honor to meet you."

He turned to her and his eyes momentarily narrowed, as if he was having trouble placing her. "Lana Hansen—as I live and breathe. It's always nice to meet someone with such important connections."

His eyes twinkled, and a smile seemed to be curling his lips. Lana stared at Chet, befuddled. Because of the article, she had expected him to act horribly towards her, but he seemed jovial. Yet what did he mean by someone with important connections? Dotty was the only person she knew who would fit that bill.

"We are fans of your guidebooks at Wanderlust Tours," Lana said.

"I had never heard of your *Travel Time* blog before your name appeared on the list as a last-minute fill-in. It's a good thing the panel brought you to my attention."

Lana blushed and mumbled her thanks.

"Your presence confirmed what I have long suspected—that this conference is being run by a bunch of corrupt souls who are more concerned with scoring freebies than promoting the best that travel writing has to offer. I have already been in contact with the organization. Your boss had no right pushing you onto this panel. By doing so, she has tarnished the integrity of the entire conference. If you choose to join the discussion, I will have no choice but to write a blog post exposing her disgraceful actions. Trust me, it will be the end of Wanderlust Tours."

"You must be lying—Dotty is as honest as they come!" Lana exclaimed.

Chet's laugh made her skin crawl. "Then why did she blackmail the organizers into including you?"

His remark stopped Lana short. Before she could think up a response, his taxi driver opened the door for him.

"If you are smart, you will skip the panel discussion," Chet said before stepping inside.

"You are a horrid man," she retorted in a far louder voice than she had meant to use. It seemed as if everyone waiting on the curbside was staring at her. She ducked her head, embarrassed that Chet had gotten to her, and raced back to her group.

Chet had better watch his back if he wants to make it through the week, she fumed internally as she made her way back inside.

Randy rushed over to her. "Is everything alright? We heard some sort of ruckus outside. Were you arguing with Chet? What did he do now?"

Lana smirked. "He threatened to destroy Wanderlust Tours in his next blog article because he thinks Dotty bribed or blackmailed someone in order to get me onto the discussion panel. As if. Dotty is a stickler for rules."

"Then don't let him get to you."

"Easier said than done," Lana replied.

She started to walk away when Randy grabbed her arm. "Hey, I read that article, too. Ouch. But if I was you, I wouldn't take what he said too personally. His tone was so whiny and negative, no one worth listening to would take his words at face value."

"You are right. I can't let Chet bother me. That is exactly what bullies want—for you to react. This is the opportunity of a lifetime, and I need to take full advantage of it," she confirmed. "Now let's get our group to the travel expo."

7

Quinoa Tofu Burgers

Lana stood at the crossroads of two wide paths stretching the length and breadth of the massive conference center. She had never seen so many travel-related companies or products before. It was like walking through a catalog. Everywhere she looked were booths and displays promoting different magazines, guidebooks, trips, and a plethora of merchandise. But then, the World Travelers Expo was arguably the most important travel and tourism trade show of the year. Lana could imagine that everyone who mattered in the industry would want to be here, hawking their wares to this crowd.

"What an incredible experience," she gushed as she admired a sun panel that folded up to the size of a credit card, yet was powerful enough to charge several electrical appliances. Randy nodded in agreement while reading through the technical specs.

Lana had never attended an international expo or conference before, but was enjoying it thoroughly. The plethora of workshops and presentations on every aspect of travel and content creation were a goldmine of knowledge. She had even attended a "Introduction to Vlogging" workshop, thinking it would be a good idea for her to also dabble in video-blogging—or vlogging. In a half hour she had learned a tremendous amount about creating high-quality videos—more than enough to realize that producing them was out of her budget for the time being.

After learning about all that was involved in the creation of a fifteen-minute video, Lana was even more in awe of Becky and Nick and their professional-looking productions. The hundreds of videos they had posted must have cost them a fortune, Lana realized, but then they were swimming in sponsors.

Being here also gave her a new respect for her boyfriend, Alex, who flew around Europe giving presentations at conferences like this one. Most of the booths that offered services were overwhelmed with interested parties, all vying for the representatives' attention. The atmosphere was high-paced and pressure-filled, yet those working the booths seemed at ease. Lana could definitely see Alex doing this kind of work; he was always so calm and collected.

Thinking about her boyfriend made her wonder what he was up to right now. He was so hard to reach lately, she sometimes flirted with the idea that he might be losing interest in her. They had been together a year in March, but were rarely in the same place because of their jobs. Yet, when she saw how busy each booth was and how those working in them were juggling several interested parties simultaneously, she understood why Alex couldn't respond to her messages or calls straight away.

The two restaurants situated within the conference hall were so busy that Lana and Randy decided to grab takeaway burgers from a vegetarian food stand and keep walking around the large conference hall until they spotted a place to sit and eat.

Their teamwork paid off after a few minutes of strolling. "Free table—on the left," Randy cried out as he darted over to a small table being vacated by another couple.

Lana hustled after her fellow guide, who already had his mouth wrapped around a quinoa tofu burger by the time she reached him. "What is your favorite gadget so far?" she asked. She unwrapped her own sandwich and took a small bite. To her surprise, it was a sensory explosion in her mouth.

He chewed his fake meat slowly, apparently contemplating his answer before responding, "It's a tough choice. The suitcases with built-in LED lights are really handy, but I'm going to have to go with the Tree Tent because

I'm going to buy one for Gloria and me."

"I saw that one, too!" Lana exclaimed. The large hammock-style tent could be strung up between multiple trees so that several campers could sleep high above the ground. "Though I don't know where you would use it in Europe. We haven't really come across many forests that you are allowed to camp in."

"That's true," Randy murmured before taking another bite of his veggie burger. "Have you seen any of our guests?" he asked through a mouthful of food.

"Only brief glimpses," Lana replied with a smile. Amber had been chatting up the makers of the Scrubba Wash, her face shining with happiness as the sales representative demonstrated how a drop of soap and liter of water could clean a small load of clothes in a matter of minutes. The portable washing machine with built-in washboard was pretty amazing and—judging from Amber's expression of joy—environmentally friendly.

Serena had been surrounded by a group of young women dressed in her line of spandex clothes, the tiny gems in the Barefoot logo on their chests dancing in the light as they all vied for the lifestyle blogger's attention. Becky and Nick had also been encircled by fans hoping for a selfie and an autograph. Even Dwight seemed to be enjoying himself; when Lana had passed by him last, he was deep in conversation with the publisher of a magazine that claimed to be the conscience of the travel industry. It sounded like a perfect fit for Dwight's style and interests.

"They all seemed happy when I saw them last," Lana added. "How about you?"

Randy chuckled. "I've only really talked to Amber. Or I should say, I listened to her fume about the flyers and the water bottles. Hopefully our talk calmed her down enough that she will leave the organizers alone."

Lana rolled her eyes. "Let me guess, they are a waste of paper and plastic?"

"Pretty much."

"You know, based on her blog, I had expected her to be more relaxed. She comes across as so low-key online. In reality, she is high maintenance."

"The aisles are littered with discarded flyers and business cards; she is right about that," Randy reasoned.

"And the cleaning crews seem to be doing a good job of sweeping them up regularly. There are so many people here, there are bound to be a few careless ones. I'm sure they will be recycled."

"Her point is they should not have been printed in the first place because it is a waste of tree pulp. Amber doesn't understand why more companies don't use digital QR codes instead of printing things on paper. I have to say that I agree with her. She might be a little militant in her attitude, but that doesn't make her wrong."

"I guess. It's just grating, the constant reminders that society isn't doing enough to save the planet. Why is she mad about the water bottles? I don't see many of those on the ground."

Randy chuckled. "Apparently she offered to gift the organization five thousand refillable bottles made of bamboo, enough for every ticket sold. Not only does she blog about the environment, she has her own line of environmentally friendly travel products, as well."

"Wow, that was really generous of her to offer. Why didn't they take her up on it?" Lana asked, wondering whether she hadn't been too harsh towards the young environmentalist.

"The organizers wanted her to pay them for the privilege, and she refused on principle."

"That doesn't make any sense."

"It's because the bamboo cups have her Green Adventures logo on them. So they considered her gift a form of sponsorship."

Lana smirked. "So it is all about the money with her."

Randy shook his head slowly. "You really don't like her, do you? Amber told me she would have happily supplied five thousand without her logo, but her network didn't have enough time to make them all. Honestly, I believe her. Her products aren't made in factories, but handcrafted by a network of local craftsmen, which means it takes more time to make them than if she had them mass-produced. But it puts the money into the locals' hands and creates new job opportunities for young people living in rural villages so they don't have to migrate to a larger city. Her heart really is in the right place, even if she's a bit fanatic."

"Huh. That is good to know. I'll try to cut her more slack," Lana mumbled and took another bite of her burger.

"Great." Randy squeezed her shoulder and smiled. A loud chiming sound filled the vast hall, reminding everyone that the next round of workshops and presentations was about to begin. Randy shoved the last of his veggie burger into his mouth, then sprung up. "There is a climbing demonstration I want to see."

Lana rose, as well. "And I'm off to see Ted's presentation."

"Okay, I'll see you by the entrance at 5 p.m., alright?"

"Sounds good. Enjoy yourself." Lana waved as Randy weaved through the dense crowd towards the large fake rock rising high above the conference room floor, before heading off to one of the smaller auditoriums for Ted's presentation.

8

Chet Ruins The Day

When Lana entered the hall, she was not certain she was in the right place until she caught sight of Ted's name splashed onto a two-story-tall screen set up behind the podium. Soon after she took a seat, one of the few still empty, the lights dimmed, and a burst of virtual fireworks went off, causing several in the audience to clap. Ted sprung up onto the stage while an upbeat rock song boomed out of the speakers.

The bombastic opening reminded Lana of how Steve Jobs announced his new Apple products. His speech was also accompanied by a series of flashy animations that illustrated how his website would function. Lana was surprised to see he had also dedicated a large portion of the site to a pay-per-read system that was almost identical to what Chet had described the first night of the conference.

Lana's eyebrows knitted together, wondering how the men would divide their audience. As much as they both pushed it as a feature the public was hungry for, readers of travel articles were a niche audience in her mind.

Luckily for Ted, he was also creating a way for freelance writers to submit new articles directly to the site—as long as they fit in with his vision of travel as a wonderous experience. As the umpteenth photo of a bikini-clad young woman dancing in the ocean's waves flashed by, Lana realized that Dwight had been right. Ted was looking for light, fluffy travel pieces and nothing too dark or sinister. There was no way that Dwight's style would ever fit in with Ted's vision.

Ted's upbeat presentation showed off his charismatic side, one Lana had not yet seen. However, his speech and slides were peppered with not-so-subtle hints that he was actively searching for sponsors, as well as content creators. Apparently his vision required quite a bit of capital to get off the ground.

The presentation of his website's features clearly struck a chord with the audience, who applauded enthusiastically for most of the half-hour-long demonstration. When Ted began wrapping his speech up, a line of interested sponsors began forming in one of the aisles. However, before Ted could finish, a commotion by the hall's entrance drew the crowd's attention.

"Don't invest in it," a familiar voice called out. "Ted stole my idea, and I'm going to shut his website down via an injunction before this conference is over!"

When Ted began sputtering a protest, Chet said loudly, "You tried to keep your little project under wraps, didn't you? Did you forget our noncompete clause?"

"That's only for products that are already live. Your website is still in the development stage, and mine will be going live next month," Ted said, holding his head up high. "You can't stop me."

"We'll see what my lawyers have to say about it," Chet said, holding his phone up for Ted to see.

Before he could dial, Ted's fiancée swatted the phone out of Chet's hand. "You can't talk to Ted like that! How dare you ruin his moment—especially after all you took from him!"

"My team has spent months perfecting my idea for a new website, which means it falls under the noncompete terms. Ted would have known that, had he run his idea past Only Footprints' legal team—as we agreed when he left the company."

"I know you screwed me over," Ted fired back. "I'm not sure yet as to how, but the forensic accountants will know soon enough."

"You signed those papers of your own free will—I didn't force you to do anything," Chet retorted.

"You didn't put a gun to my head, but you clearly took advantage of my wife's condition! Have you no shame?"

"This is business, Ted. That has always been your problem—you make everything so personal."

Ted grew red and stammered, "You can't stop me from launching my website."

"Watch me," Chet snapped and stormed off.

9

Breaking Up Is Hard To Do

"That was amazing," Lana gushed, though no one at the table could actually hear her words. The applause following the performance of *"Habanera"* from the opera *Carmen* was overwhelming.

Lana had listened to *Carmen* before she flew to Seville and had fallen in love with it. What a thrill to hear one of the most famous arias from it being performed live. The singer's voice, filled with love, passion, and a hint of sadness as she sang about her lover, brought a tear to Lana's eye. And most of her group, she noted, as Amber and Becky wiped tears from their cheeks.

The story of the naive soldier Don José being seduced by the Spanish seductress Carmen was so strongly associated with Seville that the tobacco factory where the fiery gypsy supposedly worked was still a pilgrimage site for opera fans. She hoped they would have time to visit it, too. As much as she was enjoying the travel expo, Lana was also looking forward to seeing more of the city and Andalucía in the coming days. *One more full day of this conference and then it's sightseeing time,* she reminded herself.

The delicious dinner and musical performances were the perfect way to unwind after a busy day. Tonight's party was being held in a large auditorium adjoining their hotel, where most of the travel expo attendees were staying. Everyone in her group seemed to be in good moods as they chatted about the workshops and demonstrations they'd seen.

Between performances, Lana enjoyed listening to Becky and Nick's hilarious stories about their recent adventures in Sri Lanka, so much so that she had hardly touched her food. Her full plate had nothing to do with the quality of the meal—the hotel had served a wonderful meal of *secreto ibérico*, a Spanish specialty consisting of melt-in-your-mouth pork in a thin gravy served with homemade French fries that soaked up the sauce. Luckily, they had also arranged for a vegetarian meal for Amber and Serena—*espinacas con garbanzos*—a scrumptious-looking dish made from spinach and chickpeas and served with large homemade croutons to scoop the mixture up with. Based on both women's satisfied expressions, the dish was up to snuff.

Most of all, Lana was glad that Ted and his fiancée had joined them this evening. After the disappointing end to his presentation, she wasn't sure whether they would show for dinner. He still seemed tense and slightly depressed, but far less so than directly after the presentation. Chet's accusations had put a damper on the interest of some sponsors and content creators, though a significant number had hung around to chat with Ted about his project after the drama had died down.

When Ted's phone began beeping and he rushed away from the table to answer it, his fiancée started to rise and follow before plopping back down and staring at her half-filled plate.

Was that his lawyer? Lana wondered. After today's debacle, she could imagine he would require legal advice. It didn't really matter who Ted was talking to, but her clients' happiness did. Lana took his place next to his fiancée. "Is everything okay?"

Erica pursed her lips. "No, it is most certainly not. Ted has sunk everything into this website, and Chet's thrown a gigantic wrench into his plans—again. We delayed our wedding so he could come to this conference and drum up some publicity before the site goes live, as well as secure more financial backers. Ted's plan is far grander than his budget, and I fear that without more sponsors, it is not going to get off the ground. And now Chet's threatening to get his lawyers involved. I wish we had never come here."

"Chet can't really invoke that noncompete clause if his own website is not live, can he?"

"He can certainly try. He's done it before."

"What do you mean?" Lana asked.

Erica leaned in close, obviously not wanting the others to hear her. "Chet already ruined his plan to launch a digital-only travel magazine, claiming Ted's idea was so similar to Only Footprints' blog that it violated their noncompete clause. As if that wasn't bad enough, Chet waited two months to protest Ted's idea. By that time, he had already invested thousands into the idea. And now this."

Lana shook her head. "I'm sorry—you have lost me."

When the pop band on stage launched into their next number, Erica leaned even closer, whispering in Lana's ear. "It is true that Ted tried to hide the new website from Chet. Legally speaking, he should have run it by Only Footprints' board of directors before he began working on it. But after the last fiasco, Ted figured it would be better to launch his website first, and then tell them."

Erica dabbed her eyes with a napkin before continuing. "Ted's lawyer thinks it will be difficult for Only Footprints to convince a judge that Ted should take down his live site, if theirs is still in development. But he wasn't certain and had to get back to us about it. I'm hoping that he has found the answer."

'What an awful situation," Lana murmured.

"I don't understand why Chet is out to get Ted!" Erica cried. "Since they parted ways two years ago, Chet has had the run of the board. And he had already bamboozled Ted out of his rightful share of their company when they forced him out. What more does he want?"

"Oh, I understood from Dotty that it was a mutual decision."

Erica puffed out her cheeks. "No, Chet convinced the board that Ted was unfit to continue as chief financial officer because he had been neglecting his duties for months. After Ted moved his first wife home, he refused to leave her side because he was convinced that she would wake up at any moment and he wanted to be there when she did. It took a few months before he realized that it wasn't going to happen. Before he could return to the office, the board of directors requested a meeting to discuss how they would proceed. At some point, Chet said that seeing as Ted's wife was a vegetable and he refused to pull the plug, the board could not rely on him to do his job properly."

"No," Lana gasped.

Erica grimaced. "Yes, Chet really said that. Even worse, the board agreed with him. I have never seen Ted so angry. In his severance package, they only paid him a portion of what he should have received. Chet somehow cooked the books to make it look like they were less profitable than they really were—Ted is certain of it."

"My boss did say that he and Chet had founded the company together."

"They didn't just found it together, they came up with the idea of creating the guidebooks while traveling in Europe together! Chet had always been the creative side, and Ted took care of the rest. It was thanks to Ted's connections and fundraising that they grew so exponentially the first few years. Ted poured his heart and soul into Only Footprints for twenty-eight years—he was entitled to half of the company's worth, not a fraction of it!"

What a mess, Lana thought.

Erica dabbed at her eyes again. "Chet doesn't understand why Ted did all that he did for his wife. He even called caring for her a waste of money! But then, Chet hasn't ever been married, let alone in love. I saw firsthand how much Ted cared for her. That's partly why I fell in love with him. He is one of the kindest men I have ever met."

All sorts of alarm bells began ringing in Lana's head. Did Erica and Ted have an affair while his wife was still alive? That sounded so twisted and wrong. "How exactly did you and Ted meet?"

Before Erica could answer, Ted was tapping on Lana's shoulder. "Do you mind?"

"Of course not!" Lana sprung out of his seat. Ted took his place and kissed his fiancée on the cheek.

"Good news?" Erica asked.

Ted smirked and shook his head slightly. "Not sure yet. He'll get back to me as soon as he knows more."

"Chet can't do this again!" Erica cried out as she began to tear up. Ted pulled her close.

"My lawyer will do everything he can to make certain that does not happen. Let's try to put it out of our minds for now. There is nothing else we can do but wait."

10

VIP Treatment

"Where's the man of the hour?" Dwight asked. "I don't see Sir Chet anywhere."

"He was part of a group of bigwigs that are being honored at a special performance of *Carmen* tonight. I saw them leaving together when we were waiting for our cab and asked the porter where they were off to," Amber said, sending a tinge of jealousy through Lana's body. Considering how incredible it was to hear *"Habanera,"* she could imagine it would be an almost religious experience to hear the entire opera sung in the city it was set in.

"Wow, they are really giving him the VIP treatment," Serena said.

"Thirty years is quite impressive, especially in this industry," Randy said, unaware of the wave of sadness mixed with anger that passed over Ted's face.

It must be hard for him to see Chet receive all the credit and glory, when in fact the two men founded Only Footprints and ran it for twenty-eight years as equal partners, Lana thought.

Because she was watching Ted's reaction, she almost missed seeing Serena whisper something into Dwight's ear before rising and crooking her finger at him. He sprang out of his chair and followed Serena towards the hotel's lobby without a word to the rest.

That's odd, Lana thought. Dwight had made such an abrasive first impression that she figured Serena would ignore him for the rest of the trip. *Did she have to use the restroom and wanted Dwight's help finding it?* she wondered. That didn't make much sense, but she couldn't think of another explanation.

"If anyone needs to powder their noses, there are bathrooms close to the auditorium's main entrance, on the left," Lana said to the rest. "This is a good moment to do so; they should be serving dessert in a few minutes."

"Gosh, I don't want to miss the dessert—I hear the *torrijas* are special treats for Semana Santa. Good thing we are here for Easter because I have a serious sweet tooth," Becky laughed and rose as she looked to her husband. "What about you—do you need to go?"

"Good idea." Nick smiled at the group before accompanying his wife.

"I think I'll just…" Ted said, as he sprung up and began walking towards the exit.

"I'd like to freshen up, as well," his fiancée called out.

Ted smiled as he circled back and held out his arm for his wife-to-be. As they approached the door, they crossed paths with Serena, who returned to her seat without a word.

Where was Dwight? Lana wondered. Men usually were faster when using the facilities than women. She leaned over to ask where he was just as Serena turned to Amber, blocking Lana out of her view.

"Did you see that Dani Baloney is giving a workshop on travel and Instagram activism tomorrow morning? She asked me to stop by and help her out. Would you like to join us? It could be fun."

Serena held her phone so Amber could see Dani's social media profile.

Lana's nose crinkled. *Dani Baloney—what kind of name is that? And what the heck is Instagram activism supposed to mean?*

"I love her work!" Amber squealed. "Her photo series on diving with plastic in Bali was so inspiring. I hear her pictures helped drum up the support from several companies that are now helping the locals clean up their waters. It would be an honor to share the stage with her."

Lana felt so out of touch when listening to the two young bloggers. Had she been so socially engaged when she was in her early twenties? She couldn't recall being passionate about anything global at that age. Maybe Randy was right and she should give Amber a break.

After most of their guests went off to find the toilets, Randy moved chairs to sit next to Lana. "Man, I am going to miss this."

"Miss what?" Lana asked, one eye on the group of acrobats taking the stage, as she took another sip of sangria. The fruit floating in the glass tickled her nose.

"Everything about our job, really. That's why I'm buying that hammock tent for Gloria and me. I figure we'll be doing more camping trips in Olympic National Park once I make the switch. I don't see us hanging out on our condo's balcony in the weekend. It's tiny."

Lana about choked on her drink. "What switch?"

Randy looked to her with his puppy-dog eyes. "This is going to be my last tour for a while. One of Dotty's travel agents is going on a six-month-long maternity leave a few weeks after we get back from Spain, and I'm going to fill in for her."

"What? No! You can't quit yet!" Lana blurted out. When she watched Randy and Gloria exchange their wedding vows in Italy a few months ago, Lana knew this day would come. But she figured Randy would keep working until they decided to have children. "Is Gloria pregnant?"

Randy chuckled. "Not that I'm aware of. I haven't really been home enough to make that happen, even if we wanted to start a family. It was my idea to buy that fixer-upper, and it's still a mess. When Gloria turns on the kitchen light, the garage door opens. She can't supervise all of the repairs and work full time. I'm pretty handy and can do a lot of the renovation work myself, but I haven't been home long enough to do so. Gloria put her foot down when I was back in Seattle last, and Dotty was more than accommodating. I think she saw it coming. If we work most weekends on the house, I bet we can whip it into shape before the six months is up. This way I can save us money, as well as spend more time with my wife."

Lana leaned over and hugged him tight. "I really am happy for you, but it is a shock. We've worked so many tours together this past year. I'm really going to miss you."

Randy's smile melted her heart. "Dotty's hired a lot of new recruits lately. There is bound to be someone in there that is fun to work with."

"But not as fun as you," Lana teased. "Seriously, good for you. I'm glad Dotty could make a place for you in the office."

"The timing was serendipitous, that is for certain." Randy looked around the hall as if taking it in for the first time. "I sure am going to miss working with you, too. It's great we got to come to this expo together. It almost feels like the travel industry is giving me a fantastic send-off." He laughed, but Lana saw the sadness in his eyes.

"This change isn't forever, at least if you don't want it to be. Besides, we are practically family. We'll still see each other when Alex and I are back in Seattle," Lana said.

"I hope we can get together more often than this past year. I haven't seen my big brother in months. But then, he has been extra busy with work—just like we have been."

"True," Lana said, afraid her voice might give away her despair. She had tried calling her boyfriend again last night, but he hadn't picked up. Instead, he sent a text message apologizing for being so unavailable, along with a string of kissy emojis.

In his defense, Alex had made clear that the next three weeks were going to be insanely busy because he would be working four conferences back-to-back. Which is why they had spent a long weekend in Amsterdam together before she flew to Spain. Unfortunately, Alex was so distracted by the constant stream of messages he received regarding his upcoming conferences, it did not end up being the relaxing weekend she had hoped for.

Considering the fact that her first husband had been having an affair for months before he told Lana the truth, Alex's preoccupation with his telephone had set off alarm bells in her mind. To her shame, when he had taken a long shower, she had actually checked his messages to make sure they weren't from a lover. To her enormous relief, all were work related.

Randy grimaced. "Please don't be too hard on my big brother. I know how he feels—not being able to be there as much as he would want to be. I definitely feel like that with Gloria right now."

"I get that he feels overwhelmed with work. Because two of his coworkers recently left the company, he feels pressured to help with the extra workload. But he isn't at the conference twenty-four-seven," Lana reasoned.

Randy laid his hands over hers and looked deep into her eyes. "I do know that you do not have to worry about him straying. He lights up like a Christmas tree when he talks about you, and that's all he likes to do—is talk about you. I have never seen him so in love with anyone, Lana. Not even his first wife."

Lana tried to laugh off his remark, but Randy's reassurances did help to make her feel a little better. "Thanks, Randy. But we were talking about you, not me. Do you think you will want to work as a guide again, after being home for so long?"

"That's a great question. To be honest, I had expected Gloria to apply to be a guide so we could travel Europe together and get paid for it. But being around Willow and her new baby has apparently kicked Gloria's biological clock into overdrive. She asked me last night whether we should paint the baby's room in neutral colors or gender-specific ones. I didn't know she had already picked out a room for our future offspring," Randy laughed.

"Neutral, of course," Lana chuckled along, almost ashamed to admit that she did not have the same reaction when she played with Willow's baby, Zoe. Heck, she had barely made time to visit her friend since she'd had her first child.

"I should have seen it coming," Randy said. "Gloria really wants to have a big family and doesn't want to wait too many more years before starting one. She doesn't want to be one of those mothers who has her first kid when she's forty."

Apparently realizing that Lana was ten years older than both him and Gloria, Randy blushed and added, "Of course there is nothing wrong with having kids when you are older."

Lana laughed heartily. "Don't worry—no offense taken. It's kind of strange talking with you about this, considering Alex and I haven't had this conversation yet, but I am fairly certain that your brother does not want to have kids. And I don't know if I want them, either. I'm not being a very good aunty to Willow's child. Maybe I'm not cut out to be a mom."

"Don't be hard on yourself—you would make a great mom! But you might be right about Alex. He's never been one to cuddle with the kiddies or dream about being a father. That's more of my thing."

Somehow, Randy's words saddened Lana. He apparently noticed, because he added, "But if you want children, I bet he would be open to it."

Did Alex want to have a family? She honestly did not know. Did she even want to be a mom? Lana couldn't answer that question, either. She loved her job and couldn't imagine staying home to raise a child. Would Alex?

11

No Sense of Direction

"Excuse me, but have either of you seen Ted?" Erica asked after sticking her head in between Lana and Randy.

Lana had been so engrossed with her chat that she hadn't noticed that everyone but Dwight and Ted had returned to the table.

"He wasn't waiting outside the restroom for me. I thought he might have come back here," Erica said, her voice tinged with irritation.

"Did you check your hotel room?" Randy suggested as waiters began serving their *torrijas*.

Lana was surprised to see the dessert Becky had been so enthusiastic about. It was a simple dish that appeared to be mini-slices of French toasts soaked in honey.

"He's not there, either. Where could he be?" Erica looked to the main entrance.

As much as she wanted to sample the *torrijas*, Lana followed her guest's gaze instead, just as Dwight re-entered the hall. He meandered over to the table and slipped in beside Serena, giving her a thumbs-up as he did. Serena took a sip of her water before using her phone to photograph their dessert, seemingly oblivious to Dwight's gesture.

"Have you seen Ted?" Erica asked as soon as Dwight was seated.

"No," he said, smiling serenely, "I certainly have not." He snapped open his napkin and dug into his dessert.

What had Dwight gotten up to? Lana wondered. He had been gone so long. Before she could think of a polite way to ask, Ted burst into the hall and scurried over to his fiancée.

"This place is a maze! Sorry for the delay, kitten," he said as he kissed Erica on the cheek. "I don't know how, but I got lost trying to get back to this hall."

"I'll bet," Dwight said, smiling like a Cheshire cat as he regarded Ted coyly. The older man ignored him completely.

What is Dwight's problem? Lana thought, wondering whether the two men had exchanged words when they were out of the hall. Dwight obviously wanted to work with Ted, but it was crystal clear that the feeling was not mutual.

"Where did you go?" Erica asked. "I waited for you by the bathrooms, but you never came out. I went up to our room, but you weren't there either."

"We must have just missed each other. I wanted a little privacy." He blushed slightly. "So I used the toilet in our room. But when I tried to get back to this hall, I must have taken a right when I should have gone left. Before I knew it, I was in the breakfast hall and had to ask for directions."

Lana hid her smile behind her hand. Ted had published travel guides for twenty-eight years but still managed to get lost inside of an admittedly large, but not gigantic, hotel. How did he get himself around Europe? Or was it true what the company claimed—that Chet had personally updated all of the Only Footprints travel guides?

12

Arguing Semantics

Once everyone had returned to the table, they all tucked into their dessert. Lana took a bite, and then another two in rapid succession. It was delicious. The honey-soaked bread was so soft that it literally melted in her mouth. Before she knew it, her portion was gone.

After finishing their magnificent meal, her group polished off several more pitchers of sangria while dancing the night away. Luckily, Lana and Randy didn't have to get them into a taxi, but only up to their rooms. All of her guests were able to take care of themselves—with the except of one. After he had returned from the restroom, Dwight had been strangely hyper and extra chatty, drinking far more than he had the previous night. When it was time to leave, he was having trouble walking in a straight line.

"We should escort him up to his room," Lana said.

"You're right. I hope he doesn't make a habit of this," Randy grumbled as they each grabbed one of Dwight's elbows and began propelling him towards the exit.

"Hey, what's going on?" their client exclaimed and dug in his heels.

"We're going to help you upstairs. They are closing up the hall and need everyone to leave. Okay?" Lana said in a high-pitched voice she usually reserved for small children.

Dwight relaxed his muscles, allowing them to push him along. As they maneuvered him towards the elevator, he began whistling a tune, horribly off-key.

An older couple, also waiting for the lift, eyed him warily.

When the elevator arrived and the doors opened, Lana whispered in her guest's ear. "Hey, Dwight, could you tone it down?"

"No! I'm tired of people telling me to shut up or go away. They don't notice me, but I see what they are up to. Nothing gets past old Dwight," he slurred before launching into another song.

Randy rolled his eyes while Lana apologized profusely to the others, willing the elevator to go faster.

After they half-dragged Dwight to his door, Randy fished the key card out of their client's pocket. "I'll get him into bed. As far as I'm concerned, you are free for the night."

Lana slapped him lightly on the back. "Thanks, Randy. I'll just confirm our cab for the morning and them I'm going to hit the sack. Sleep well, my friend."

"You, too," he called out as he half-carried Dwight into his room.

When Lana bounced down to the lobby, looking forward to getting this over with and crawling into bed, an angry voice wafted up the staircase. She slowed her steps and crept around the corner.

Chet was leaning over the hotel's reception desk and jabbing a finger close to the receptionist's shoulder as he continued his tirade. Three other hotel employees looked on, a pained expression gracing all of their faces.

"Great," Lana mumbled. "At least it's not one of my guests."

"How could you let something like this happen? These key cards are supposed to be safer than a lock. So how did the burglars get inside?" Chet was screaming so loudly that Lana wouldn't be surprised if people outside on the street could hear him.

"Sir, you said yourself that nothing was taken," a small man with a name tag that read "Manager" said in a calm, yet strained voice.

"Are you arguing semantics with me?" Chet shrieked. "My room has been ransacked. Did you forget that creepy note? I am not staying in that room. Someone must have stolen my key card or made a copy of it. I wouldn't be surprised if it was an employee of this hotel." Chet folded his arms firmly over his torso, almost daring the hotel's manager to contradict him.

Lana stood frozen on the last step as she listened to Chet's tirade. *What the heck happened?* Considering his extreme state, she had no interest in getting involved in this conversation. Just as she began to retreat up the staircase, he heard her footsteps and whipped around to face her.

"Oh, it's you again. You know who did this, don't you?" Chet snarled.

"Did what?" she asked, feigning innocence. The lobby was full with conference participants. Why did Chet assume that she knew something more about his room being broken into?

When the hotel's phone rang, the manager immediately grabbed the receiver. After listening for a moment, he turned to Chet. "Sir, the police wish to speak to you. Why don't you take this call in my office? It's more private."

"I'll get whoever did this, mark my words!" Chet's threat echoed through the full lobby as he followed the manager into the office.

13

Watch Your Back

April 10—Day Three of the World Travelers Expo in Seville, Spain

"Did everyone hear about the break-in last night?" Serena asked in a loud whisper as she leaned over the table and held up her phone. Lana could see that Serena's Twitter account was open, but she couldn't read the tweet from where she was sitting.

Ted and his fiancée exchanged perplexed glances with Becky and Nick.

"What break-in?" Erica asked.

Amber barely looked up from her phone. From what Lana could see, the environmental blogger was checking her own social media feeds.

"Chet's hotel room was broken into last night," Serena continued.

Erica gasped and clutched at her chest. "That's horrible! How did they get in? Do we need to worry, too, Ted?"

Her fiancé blushed brightly as he stuttered, "No, there's no need to worry. I bet it's a publicity stunt. I wouldn't put it past Chet to do something like that."

"He tweeted photos of his room and the note the thieves left. Whoever did it, they sure made a mess of things." Serena chortled as she glanced again at the photos on her phone before passing it around.

"'Watch your back'—real original," Becky laughed.

"I wonder who did it," Dwight said when it was his turn to view Chet's

Twitter feed. "I bet they will be in lots of trouble." He looked up at Ted and winked.

Ted laughed nervously. "I guess they will." He craned his neck to see the screen in Dwight's hand. "Gosh, they even cut up his bowties. Wow, someone really doesn't like Chet."

When the phone reached Lana, she was shocked to see the level of destruction. Looking at the pictures of Chet's room turned her stomach. It had been torn to shreds. Whoever did this was full of anger. Not only were his clothes cut up or slashed, but all of his toiletries had been smashed onto the bathroom floor as well. What creeped Lana out the most was the note the intruder had left on his pillow. "Watch your back" was written in bright pink lipstick on a sheet of hotel stationery. Its placement somehow made the simple message even more intimate and threatening.

Lana looked to her female guests' lips but didn't see the same color on any of theirs. *Not that that clears them of the crime*, she thought. Anyone could have picked up a lipstick in the hotel's extensive gift shop—even one of the men.

She suddenly glanced at Ted and Dwight, then looked away as quickly, hoping they could not read her thoughts. Maybe Chet was right and she did know who had done this. Both men knew Chet was at the opera, and they were both gone from the table for quite a long time last night. Either would have had time to ransack Chet's room. But how did they get in? As far as she knew, neither was a master thief. More importantly, why would either do something so stupid as breaking into another conference participant's room? There were so many people milling about at all hours, the chances of getting caught red-handed were quite high.

When her hand began to vibrate, signaling a new text message, Lana realized that she still was still holding Serena's phone. She turned to Amber so as to pass it along, but the younger woman waved it away.

"I've already seen the photos, thanks. It looks like karmic payback to me. That dinosaur got exactly what he deserves. But Chet's room is not important." Amber leaned in towards the group. "The discussion panel this afternoon is. We can't let him get away with those offensive remarks he made in his blog. So what are we going to do about it?"

"I say we take the higher road and ignore the article—as well as Chet. Besides, I bet someone in the audience will ask him about it. His article has made quite a sensation in the travel press. Any journalist worth their salt would smell a story," Serena said.

Amber was silent a moment, apparently taking in Serena's suggestion. "You have a point. None of us should react if we are questioned about the article, even if Chet brings it up himself. The more we ignore him, the more upset he will become. He's bound to say something mean-spirited and embarrass himself."

Serena nodded sharply. "Exactly. As my granddad used to say, if you give a fool enough rope, he'll hang himself."

14

A Good Day

"Is everyone excited about the panel discussion? I can't wait to hear what you all say," Randy enthused, grinning at his guests.

"We can't wait, can we, hon? I feel most in my element when we are in front of the camera," Becky glowed.

"Becky is a natural," Nick said as he squeezed his wife's hand. "It was her idea to start shooting videos, and it was the best business decision we ever made. Since we started posting them, our popularity has increased dramatically."

Dwight chuckled when Nick said "business decision," but the vlogging duo ignored him. Most of her guests did tend to snub Dwight, Lana realized. Only Serena had shown interest in him yesterday, but that was fleeting. Today she seemed to be avoiding his attempts at conversation again.

"It sounds like a lot of my followers are going to be attending," Serena said to Amber. "At least they say they are going to be in the audience. I wonder how many will actually show up."

"Could you share my eMagazine on your social media before you speak on the panel? That way I can take advantage of your spike in views," Dwight said, pushing his way into their conversation again.

Serena pursed her lips but didn't make eye contact with him. "We'll see."

"Oh, that's a great idea," Amber enthused. "I'm going to ask my followers if any are planning on watching the discussion today. I should share the link to the livestream while I'm at it," she said, then turned her attention back to her phone. Seconds later, her fingers were flying over the tiny keyboard.

Lana glanced at her clock and noticed that the taxi would soon be arriving. "Folks, our ride should be here in about ten minutes, which should give us enough time for another coffee or tea. Any takers?"

She looked to Dwight, the person sitting closest to her.

"No, thanks. Say, Ted, can I talk with you for a moment? I have a business proposal for you."

Ted looked puzzled. "If it's about a freelance job again, I thought I was pretty clear yesterday. Your style just isn't what we are looking for."

Dwight stood and leaned over the older man. "Trust me, you are going to want to hear this. Why don't we step away from the table so we can talk more privately?"

When Ted began to protest, Dwight chuckled. "What's wrong—are you too tired from your little adventure last night?"

Ted's frown deepened. "Do you mean the party?"

Dwight shook his head and moved in closer. Whatever Dwight said to Ted, it made the older man go white and follow Dwight away from the group.

So Ted was the break-in artist, Lana assumed. Lordy, what a nightmare. Had Dwight seen Ted enter or exit Chet's room? But why would Dwight have been up in the hotel's hallway at that moment? Had he preferred the privacy of his own room's bathroom over a public toilet? Or had he also intended to try to get into Chet's room and Ted beat him to it?

But what would either man have achieved by doing so? Were they looking for something or simply trying to scare Chet into leaving the conference?

While Lana's thoughts had been wandering, Randy had been fulfilling their guests' drink orders. Just as he returned to the table with the three requested coffees, the hotel's receptionist bounded up to the group. "Your taxi is here. He is a few minutes early; shall I ask him to wait?" she added when she noted the fresh drinks.

Lana looked to her group, most of whom were already rising. "No, I think we are ready to go."

She glanced around the lobby and spotted Ted and Dwight in the far corner, talking animatedly. Whatever Dwight was telling him, the older man did not look pleased to hear it.

Figuring Ted would welcome the intrusion, Lana dashed over, calling out to them as she did. "Sorry to interrupt, but our taxi is here."

Ted all but ran to the hotel's exit and into the awaiting cab. Dwight followed at a more leisurely pace, whistling softly as he did.

"Everything okay?" Lana asked as he crossed her path.

Dwight winked at her before slapping her back as if they were old friends. "More than okay. Today is shaping up to be a good day for Dwight Anderson."

15

He Said, She Said

"You can do this," Lana mumbled under her breath as she forced her legs to keep walking towards the large auditorium where the panel discussion was being held. Her stomach had begun flip-flopping long before her phone's alarm beeped, alerting her to the upcoming event. The closer it got to start time, the more harried and inexperienced she felt.

Everyone in her group had wanted to visit the conference on their own before the panel discussion began at three. Lana had spent the morning walking around the expo hall in a daze, half listening to a variety of product demonstrators hawking their wares until her phone's alarm vibrated in her pocket. Although she didn't feel mentally prepared, there was no going back. Despite Chet's threats to badmouth Wanderlust Tours on his blog, Lana knew that Dotty would never forgive her if she canceled at the last minute.

She had asked Randy to have lunch with her again, hoping it would help calm her nerves. But he and Gloria had been up all night discussing whether or not to remove a wall in their new condo's living room. During their quick meal, his eyelids kept fluttering shut. Lana only hoped that the panel discussion would be interesting enough to keep him awake. It was going to be a long and intense three hours—for her anyway.

During her wanderings today, she had spotted all of her group members but hadn't caught a single glimpse of Chet Rogers. *Maybe he decided not to come to the panel discussion,* she dared to hope.

When she approached the auditorium's entrance, her eyes widened as she took in the long line of attendees waiting to enter. Walking along it, shaking hands and signing autographs, were Becky and Nick Soho. Lana knew they were popular, but she had not expected them to have so many admiring fans. *No wonder a television network is interested in them,* she thought.

When she entered the space, her eyes were drawn to a large screen hanging on the back wall, upon which her face and blog's masthead—along with the other six participants'—were projected. She gulped as the reality of what she was about to do sank in.

In front of the screen was a table stretching across the podium, the seven chairs placed behind it lit up in the spotlights. Name cards were placed before each chair. The rest of the panelists—with the exception of the Sohos—were already seated.

In the center of the table sat Chet, preening like a peacock as a gaggle of reporters questioned him for their magazines, radio stations, and travel channels. Lana was still surprised that he showed up, given that all of the targets in his blog post were now seated alongside him.

His three-piece suit and bowtie were quite the contrast to the rest of the panel, clothed in far more casual attire. *His clothing is symbolic of his role on this panel*, Lana thought. The rest of the panelists were representatives of the new generation, and their way of communicating differed greatly from Chet's. *That must be difficult for him to accept*, Lana realized, as she caught herself almost feeling sorry for him. However, as soon as his article flashed through her mind, her empathy disappeared.

Lana took her place at the table, sandwiched between Becky's empty seat and Serena. The lifestyle blogger smiled a hello then returned her attention to her phone. From what she could see, Serena was responding to comments left on her social media.

The plethora of cameras pointed at the podium made Lana nervous. It seemed as if all of the world's travel channels were in attendance. She knew that this discussion was being broadcast into the conference center's main hall as well as streamed live online so that virtual participants could also attend it. But she had not expected to see so many cameras and microphones pointed at them.

She then looked out over the vast auditorium and two tiers of seating. Officially this space could seat five hundred, and based on the long lines of attendees filing inside, every seat was going to be filled.

Lana tried to ignore the multitude of cameras, as well as the vastness of the auditorium. *Pick a random person in the middle of the hall and pretend like you are talking only to them* was her mother's advice. It had sounded much easier back in Seattle.

Originally she'd thought that speaking on this panel would not be a problem. After all, she had spent several years touring the United States as The Great Ronaldo's assistant and was used to being on stage and in the spotlight. Yet speaking to an audience of thousands was quite different than being the assistant to a magician. She and her ex-husband, The Great Ronaldo, had performed and rehearsed their act so many times that she could do it in her sleep. And during his shows, no guests were interested in hearing her opinions. All they wanted to see was her smiling coyly and acting surprised when the acts worked.

Before her growing nervousness could overwhelm her, Gabriela Morales, a popular Spanish television personality who was acting as moderator for this event, darted over to Lana and stuck out her hand. "We are thrilled you are able to join us today, even on such short notice."

"My pleasure. It was perfectly timed, seeing as I was already leading the tour to Seville. Thanks for inviting me to speak," Lana gushed.

A tight smile passed over Gabriela's face. "Yes, well, as the newest blogger on this panel, we want to hear your thoughts on the future of travel writing, as well as your recommendations for creating the perfect blog post. You have a good grasp of photo-rich content and the importance of keeping your textual descriptions brief. I think it is exactly what contemporary travelers are looking for—bite-sized posts that inspire them to learn more about a place or culture. That's a winning combination, if you ask me."

Her enthusiasm was infectious. Lana felt herself smiling and her nerves subsiding as her grimace relaxed into a smile. "Hey, thanks."

The bubbly moderator sprung up as soon as Becky and Nick stepped onto the podium. Gabriela gave them approximately the same warm introduction as Lana, then wished them luck before rushing offstage.

Seconds later, the doors closed, and the lights dimmed. Gabriela walked back out onto the stage and into the spotlights, her arms wide open, as if she was welcoming everyone with a hug.

"*Hōla* and welcome to this year's World Travelers Expo in Seville! It is a joy to see so many visitors interested in listening in on our panel discussion today, both in this auditorium and online." Gabriela's voice boomed through the speakers. She gestured towards the cameras pointing at the panelists and smiled even more broadly.

"Before we discuss the future of travel writing, let us meet our panelists—all of whom bring a unique perspective to this conversation."

She moved so that she was standing just behind Chet. "Let us begin with our oldest and perhaps most esteemed speaker today—Chet Rogers, founder and CEO of Only Footprints guidebooks."

Chet rose as a polite applause filled the hall.

"Thank you," he said, his high-pitched voice squeaking through the microphone as he adjusted his bowtie. "It is wonderful to meet so many readers. I am thrilled to represent the—"

"Mr. Rogers will be bringing thirty years of insight into travel writing to our discussion today," Gabriela said, talking over Chet, to his obvious irritation.

She walked over to the Sohos. "Next, we have the creators of the *Life's A Journey* blog and video subscription channel—Becky and Nick Soho!"

The deafening applause brought Lana's fingers over her ears. Chet must have realized the audience's response was even louder for them, because he was reddening quite fast.

"It sounds like we have many of their fans in our audience!" Gabriela cried out, garnering another round of hoots and claps. "Their creative travel videos have made them some of the world's most popular travel bloggers for the past three years running."

The Sohos rose from their seats and waved enthusiastically to the audience. "Thanks so much for following along on our journeys!" Becky cried out.

"And sitting next to them is our newest blogger, Lana Hansen. She posts to her *Travel Time* blog about adventures she has while working as a guide for Wanderlust Tours, a high-end tour company based out of Seattle, Washington."

A smattering of polite applause followed, to Lana's delight. Considering how few followers she had in comparison to the rest of the panelists, she had feared her introduction would be met with silence.

"The gorgeous lady on Lana's right is no other than Serena Tan, lifestyle blogger extraordinaire and, coincidentally, a good friend of mine." Gabriela leaned down to kiss Serena on the cheek.

Many of the millennials stood up and began hooting enthusiastically, the glittery footprint logos on their clothing dancing in the lights. Shrieks of delight filled the auditorium when Serena blew kisses to the audience and called out, "I see you all sparkling!"

"Sitting next to Serena is Amber Laurent, founder of Green Adventures Eco-products and the creative mind behind the *Lessen Your Carbon Footprint* blog."

Amber also had a good following in the crowd, based on the claps she received.

"And last, but certainly not least, we are honored to have Ted Castle joining us today."

Ted puffed out his chest at the introduction, then rose and bowed to the crowd. Erica shot up from her seat in the front row, clapping loudly and longer than those around her—almost embarrassingly so.

"I hear his new website is going to revolutionize how we read and write about travel! It sure sounds like Ted is about to give traditional travel guides such as Only Footprints a run for their money," Gabriela laughed as Chet turned an even deeper shade of crimson. "Which is interesting considering Ted was one of the original founders. I can't wait to hear his perspective on our first statement."

She gestured towards the screen behind her, and the two statements they were to discuss appeared on it. The first was "The future of travel writing is online—not in print." Underneath it was "Content creators are morally obliged to promote sustainable and environmentally friendly ways of travel."

"Today we are going to listen to our esteemed panel debate these two topics before opening up the floor to your questions and comments."

She turned and winked at the seven panelists, all watching her intently. "Okay, panel, are you ready to get started?"

When Lana nodded, a nervous giggle escaped her throat.

The crowd burst into applause.

"Ted, would you like to begin?"

16

More Questions Than Answers

An hour later, Lana was completely drained. What should have been a civil discussion had gone from friendly to cutthroat almost immediately. Chet used every opportunity to cut down or denigrate what the others said, to the point that the bubbly moderator began cutting off his responses so as to give the others a chance to share their thoughts uninterrupted. Unfortunately, her actions only made Chet grow even more blusterous and negative.

What is his long game? Lana wondered. It was a mystery to her as to why Chet thought it was okay to act so rudely during this discussion. Not only were there hundreds of people watching in the auditorium, there were apparently thousands more watching via livestream. Considering the cameras' presence, Lana figured he would have been on his best behavior.

After an intense first hour, Lana could tell the rest of the panel was as restless as she was, and they had only gotten through the two prepared statements. Yet she didn't dare stand up and stretch, not with the cameras pointed at them.

"Who wants to take a five-minute break before we begin with the question-and-answer session?" the moderator asked, as if she had been reading Lana's mind. A murmur of approval arose from the auditorium as most of the panelists and several audience members began to rise.

That is, until Chet laughed loudly into his microphone. "Are you serious? A real traveler should be able to sit for hours in a bus, train, or plane without being able to stretch their legs. Let's forget that nonsense and continue our discussion. It has been intellectually stimulating so far, and I am curious to hear from our audience."

Lana suppressed a snort. All Chet had done so far was put down his fellow panelists, dismissing almost everything they had said as nonsense. It was grating on Lana's nerves and, based on her fellow panelists' expressions, she wasn't the only one irritated by his rudeness.

Was he always so ill-mannered? Or was he trying to prove to the audience that he and his printed guidebooks were still relevant, as Dotty suspected? If that was his master plan, then it was backfiring spectacularly. Based on the audience's reactions so far, no one seemed particularly interested in what he had to say. Though Lana did notice that the average age of the seated public was probably thirty, and thus far younger than Chet's target audience.

A long line was forming at the microphone, placed in the middle of the center aisle. The first question came from a twenty-something woman wearing a flowery sundress. "My question is for Amber Laurent," she said, causing the blogger in question to smile and nod encouragingly.

"I am such a fan of your blog! You really make me aware of how we can make small changes that truly help the environment. There is no Planet B, is there?" A round of applause followed, making the blogger blush, before the audience member continued.

"I'm heading to Cambodia and Laos next month. I wondered if you had any advice for slow travel routes through that part of Asia."

"Certainly," Amber said and leaned into her microphone. "I also have several slow travel routes and transportation options listed on my website. There is a great route along the Mekong River that takes you through Laos, Thailand, and Cambodia."

Before Amber could elaborate, Chet sniggered and mumbled into his microphone, "After you fly there first. Amber's blog should not be called *Lessen Your Carbon Footprint*, but rather *How to Leave a Massive One*. According to her social media, she's flown to ten countries this past month alone! How many trees do you have to plant to compensate for that amount of air travel, hmm?" Chet sneered at Amber, but the young lady's composure didn't waver.

"I truly believe that broadening your mind and horizons are compensation enough for the extra carbon emissions," she retorted. "But you are right, I was quite busy this past month flying to ten locations around the Pacific Ring. I was planning on keeping the reason a surprise, but since Chet has spoilt that…" She turned back to the crowd. "I am happy to announce the opening of ten new wildlife rescue and rehabilitation clinics in Southeast Asia. All will be fully staffed by local experts, equipped with the latest medical devices available, and ready to accept all furry and feathered clients indigenous to that region. Local farmers will profit the most, as they can bring their livestock to any of our clinics and use our veterinary services for free. It's travelers like you that made this possible—all of the profits from my Green Adventure eco-products will be used to fund more centers like these."

Her words were greeted with a standing ovation, one Lana spontaneously found herself taking part in.

What a classy young lady, Lana thought. Not only for handling Chet with such finesse, but also for dedicating her business profits to helping the planet. The young lady wasn't simply regurgitating what she thought her peers wanted to hear—she was truly practicing what she preached. Lana had totally pegged Amber wrong.

"If you go to my Green Adventures website, you can learn more about the centers, as well as donate or sign up to volunteer at several charities around the world. Be part of the solution," she exclaimed once the applause died down.

When Chet pulled a nasty face and leaned into his microphone, Amber rushed to add, "If you do have the time, I strongly recommend volunteering at a local charity or school for at least a few weeks. Housing is usually included in the volunteer fees, and living with locals is a wonderful way to learn more about their country and culture. Far more than flying into a city, staying at posh hotels, and only taking organized tours."

Chet turned red and started to sputter a response when the moderator pointed to the microphone in the center of the auditorium. "Thank you for asking about slow travel. Who's next?"

The next audience member to pose a question was clearly a fan of the Sohos. The young woman was giggling and blushing so much she could barely finish asking her question. "I just love your videos. They so inspire me to visit places I never would have considered, otherwise. Watching them is so much better than reading about a place, you know what I mean? So I just, like, want to thank you for posting them. You guys should totally be on TV! Can you see yourselves hosting a travel show one day, or do you prefer the freedom of posting to your own channel?"

Becky and Nick looked to each other and smiled. "It would be wonderful to see us on TV, wouldn't it? We will have to wait and see what happens," Becky responded cryptically, before adding, "That is all I can say for now."

"Videos are not as important as guidebooks," Chet said dismissively. "Books are what people actually pack and use during their trip."

"Maybe in the past, but me and my friends prefer to read eBooks on our smartphones. They take up way less space. And videos give me a better feel for a place than a book does," the young woman at the mic said, bringing a sneer to Chet's face.

"You know that saying, 'a book is always better than the film'? You could say the same about travel," he retorted. "Videos are not as long-lasting as a published book because they are quickly outdated and cannot be easily updated. Videos should add to the brand, but should not be the only product."

What is with that guy? Lana wondered again. He had spent the past hour putting his fellow panelists down, and for seemingly no reason other than out of spite. And now he was butting in on other people's questions in order to do the same.

"I, too, am in negotiations with a television production company for a travel show. However, mine will add to the Only Footprints brand, not replace my information-rich guidebooks," he continued in his contemptuous tone.

"Oh yeah?" the young woman standing at the microphone responded politely as Becky and Nick exchanged worried glances.

"When is yours airing?" the audience member asked.

"As soon as a legal issue is sorted out," Chet said and shot Becky and Nick a wicked grin before returning his attention to the vast public.

Although he was addressing the giggling woman at the microphone, it was Becky and Nick who seemed to be reacting more than anyone else. Both vloggers went as white as sheets, their eyes wide as they stared at Chet. *Why would Becky or Nick care what Chet was up to?* Lana wondered.

Becky held her hand over her microphone and stammered, "You can't weasel your way back in."

Chet leaned over Lana to make eye contact with the Sohos. "I guess it depends on how good your agent is. We will just have to wait and see how it all plays out, won't we?"

"Thank you," the moderator said to the audience member, seemingly oblivious to the staring contest taking place on stage. "What is our next question?"

The next forty minutes were filled with questions about Ted's website and the Sohos' advice for beginning vloggers. Sensing that the public wasn't interested in her opinions, Lana poured a large glass of sparkling water and leaned back in her chair.

After Amber answered a long-winded question about sustainable travel options, Dwight approached the microphone. Lana had trouble placing the expression on his face. Was it smugness or satisfaction? When he stepped into the spotlight, Chet tensed up visibly, then looked away.

Considering the extra attention Chet had been receiving during the conference so far, Lana had expected more audience members to have a question for him. So far, there had been none. Yet, based on Chet's physical response, he was not looking forward to answering one if it was posed by Dwight.

"Mr. Rogers, you claim to write all of your travel guides yourself—including the biannual updates." Dwight's tone was formal, as if they had never met.

"I don't claim anything—I pride myself on doing so," Chet roared.

Lana's eyebrows knitted together. While his claim that he had written all of the original guides himself was plausible, it was hard to believe he had kept up with all of the biannual updates. There were thousands of hotels, restaurants, and tourist sites described in each guide. It was virtually impossible for one person to do so—even if they were traveling around Europe full time. So why did he keep up the pretense and defend the absurd claim so heavily?

"Really?" Dwight held a small notebook close to the microphone as he flipped through it, causing a rattling noise to resound through the speakers. "Then why are all the notes for the latest Bulgaria updates in my handwriting?"

Chet sprung out of his chair and pointed a finger at Dwight. "Thief! Those notes were stolen from my office months ago. Security—I want that man arrested!"

"What? That's not true! Look for yourself—my handwriting fills these pages, not his. You are a fraud who cheats writers out of their bylines!" Dwight screamed as two burly security guards closed in on him.

"Don't listen to him!" Chet yelled. "Those notes are my property—not his! Take that notebook away from him!"

"No!" Dwight screamed and pulled the notebook to his chest, wrapping his arms tightly around it.

The two guards lifted Dwight by the elbows and dragged him, kicking and screaming, out of the hall. "Watch your back, old man, because I'm coming for you! You can't get away with this!"

Lana half rose from her chair, unsure whether her duties as tour guide took precedence over her place on the panel. Only when she saw Randy scamper after the security guard did she relax back into her chair.

The auditorium was as silent as a grave, as if everyone was having trouble processing what had just happened.

Only one person seemed unaffected. Chet flicked a piece of lint off of his shirt, then asked, "Where were we?"

Gabriela was momentarily ruffled, but she recovered her composure quickly. "Um, we have another question."

The young brunette standing in front of the microphone was dressed in spandex tights underneath a loose-fitting tunic, which was emblazoned with a short phrase. From where she was seated, all Lana could read was the text "Take Pictures."

"Hi, I have a wardrobe question for Serena. By the way, I love your new clothing line! I attend a lot of yoga and Pilates workshops around the world. Would you recommend drying spandex on a retractable clothesline strung out over a balcony overnight, or is it better to hang it over a chair inside of my hotel room?"

Lana wanted to roll her eyes, but the young woman's serious expression made clear that she really wanted to know the answer.

Serena leaned forward into her microphone, nodding thoughtfully. "Excellent question. I don't recommend either one. The damp fabric may damage a chair's varnish. And though I would hang clothes outside during the day, at nighttime be sure to bring them inside. There are lots of insects and other little critters that love to curl up in the damp fabric—that's an unpleasant surprise in the morning," she chuckled, getting a rise out of the audience.

"A better idea would be to use your hotel room's shower curtain rod or to string up a clothesline in the bathroom and use clothespins to hang your clothes up. The fabric dries much faster when it is not folded. Don't forget to download the packing list from my Barefoot Travel website before you go—clothespins are on it specifically for that reason. They take up so little space and are so practical and versatile. I have a whole list of things you can use them for on my website, as well."

Murmurs of approval and ticking noises reverberated through the hall as many of the audience members presumably typed into their phones either Serena's words of wisdom or her website's address.

"Great advice, as always," Gabriela gushed. "What is our next question?"

When the young woman stepped away from the microphone, the text on her shirt was suddenly visible.

"Wait a moment, what does your T-shirt say?" Chet asked, squinting as he rose to better see the text.

"'Take only pictures, leave only footprints'—it's the motto of Serena's clothing line, Barefoot Travel."

Chet slammed his palm against his forehead, then glared at the lifestyle blogger. "You can't be serious! How did you manage to mangle that, Serena? It's 'take only memories, leave only footprints.' Not pictures! Chief Seattle said that. It means you leave beautiful places as you found them! That's why that quote is printed on the back of all of my guidebooks and the reason why we are called Only Footprints. Are you stealing my motto now, as well as my logo? Have you no shame?"

"Are you blind?" Serena snapped, momentarily blowing her chill cover. "Our logos and brand names are completely different."

"We'll see what the judge has to say," Chet countered.

Lana admired Serena's persistence, but to her, the two brands did look awfully similar. Not only was the footprint they both used as their logo identical, the font Serena used for her Barefoot Travel brand name was the same as Only Footprints.

"Okay, folks. We have wandered way off topic," Gabriela said. "Ladies and gentlemen, I think it is time to wrap up this stimulating discussion. I wish to thank you all for coming to—"

"Wait! I have a question for Chet Rogers," a middle-aged woman yelled as she pushed her way to the front of the line of audience members waiting at the microphone. Her voice had a lovely Spanish lilt to it.

"Let her speak," Chet announced loudly as he sat up straighter.

"I have read many of your blog posts and articles, but your last post was mean and completely unprofessional. Why did you launch a smear campaign against the other panelists days before this discussion was to take place? This is not the first time you have used written words to spread slanderous remarks about an honest business owner."

The woman's statement was met with a burst of applause, momentarily lifting Lana's spirits. *Someone finally dared to stand up to Chet Rogers*, she thought.

Lana's surge of euphoria dissipated as soon as Chet responded, his chin jutted up in the air.

"Because they deserve it. I meant every word I wrote. I have been in this business for thirty years and have seen all sorts come and go. No one else on this panel will last as long as I have, mark my words."

"Hang on there," Ted began to sputter, but his former business partner ignored him.

Instead, Chet squinted to see the woman at the microphone better, holding a hand over his eyes to block out the spotlights. "Josepha? Is that you?"

Instead of answering, the woman darted out of the spotlight and raced out of the hall.

17

Car Trouble

Precisely three hours after the panel discussion began, Gabriela announced that they were closing the floor to questions.

"I want to thank all of the panelists and our wonderful audience for the lively conversation. Give yourselves a round of applause—you deserve it!" she cried into the microphone, causing the public and panelists to rise and cheer. It was a great way to put a positive spin on the rocky end to the discussion, Lana thought as she rose and joined in.

She was mentally exhausted from keeping up with the questions and debate. No one had asked her a direct question, which was not odd considering who the other panelists were. But it was still a tad disappointing. *Hopefully my presence on this panel was enough to help increase my blog's popularity,* she thought.

Luckily, she didn't have to deal with the Dwight situation straight away. Randy had already messaged to let her know that he inquired about their guest. The conference center's security staff did not have the authority or a reason to actually arrest Dwight—as Lana feared they would—but had removed him from the hall because he was disrupting the panel discussion. According to Randy's message, they had kept Dwight in their office until the event was finished because he continued to make threats towards Chet and they didn't want him interrupting the discussion again. Now that it was over, Randy was free to pick him up.

Lana breathed a sigh of relief. The security staff had gotten Dwight out of there so fast, she was slightly concerned they had taken him straight to jail. It would be nice to lead a tour that did not include a visit to the local police station.

As fatigued as she was, Lana was really looking forward to the upcoming dinner and flamenco workshop—an evening of entertainment specially arranged for the panelists and a small number of VIPs attending the conference. Dotty had also secured tickets for Dwight and Randy, meaning their entire tour group would be present. Being one of the travel expo's main sponsors apparently had its benefits.

After Gabriela had officially closed the discussion, she approached the panelists. "You were all wonderful. Thank you for joining us today." She beamed her perfect smile at all seven of them. "Several reporters have requested a few more minutes of your time. When you are finished talking with them, a taxi will take you all to the theater."

"What a great experience." Becky sprung up and gave Gabriela a quick hug before stretching out her back. "I can't wait to move around after that! If you don't mind, Nick and I would prefer to walk over to the theater after we talk to the media."

The moderator's grin faltered. "Are you certain?"

"It's only a short walk from here. Becky and I want to get our blood pumping before we sit down again to eat," Nick explained.

Curious to know more about their strong reactions to Chet's comments, as well as spend a little time with her blogging heroes, Lana piped up, "I do, too. Would you mind if I joined you?"

"Of course not," Becky said and squeezed her shoulder, making Lana's night.

Serena raised a finger at Gabriela. "I would prefer the taxi."

"As would I," Chet said, his tone strangely aggressive.

He must still be worked up over the questions—or the lack of—that he received during the Q&A session, Lana assumed.

Ted turned to Gabriela. "We appreciate the offer, but Erica and I will ride over in a separate car. We have no desire to spend another second with that awful man."

"Can you afford it?" Chet asked with a laugh. "From what I hear, you don't have much of an expense account to play with. Are you certain you don't want to accept the free ride?"

Why do Chet's eyes twinkle when he is being malicious? Lana thought. It was quite unbecoming.

Serena laid a hand on Ted's arm. "Why don't we ride over together—my treat?"

"That is gracious of you," Ted said as he bowed slightly towards Serena.

"Care to join us, Amber?"

The young environmentalist nodded. "Love to, thanks." She held out an elbow and Serena hooked her arm through it. The pair swept over to the awaiting press corps and smiled brightly while each answered a reporter's question.

"Do you want to talk with the reporters, too?" Erica asked her fiancé.

Before Ted could reply, Chet darted over to the awaiting media.

Ted's lips pursed as he watched his old business partner smile for the cameras. "No, I'm good for now. It's been a long day, and there is another networking event tomorrow."

The couple watched as Amber and Serena wrapped up their answers and waved goodbye to the reporters before walking towards the exit, without a single glance towards Chet.

Becky and Nick, however, were not going to let Chet's presence spoil their chance to talk to the media. They sauntered over to the press and were immediately inundated with questions.

Knowing that Randy would take Dwight straight to the theater after he'd picked their client up from the security office, Lana moved closer to better hear how Chet, Becky, and Nick fielded questions for the few reporters still remaining.

Yet Chet's moment in the sun was short-lived. Several reporters' questions about the mean-spirited comments he had made during the discussion, as well as his blog article, had him cursing the media out in no time flat.

"It's because of you that trend-hoppers like them are popular," Chet raged at the cameras while pointing at Becky and Nick. "You all have the attention span of a gnat—try reading a book for a change!"

Chet turned away from the reporters and pointed at Gabriela. "You—take me to the taxi!" he barked before storming off towards the auditorium's exit.

18

The Secret to Their Success

After Chet's hissy fit, the reporters turned their cameras on Becky and Nick. The duo gracefully circumvented questions about Chet's offensive comments, instead subtly promoting their blog, website, and video channel in a positive and uplifting way.

Lana was in awe. *No wonder they are so successful.* When the duo waved goodbye to the television crews and reporters, Lana tagged along behind them. The conference center was still abuzz with those visiting the trade show, attending workshops, or waiting for the evening's networking events to begin.

After they'd weaved through the dense crowds of conference participants and were out on the streets, Lana breathed in the warm air and gazed around at her surroundings. The city was awash in sunlight. Bushy orange trees lined the streets—their deep-green leaves contrasted wonderfully with the buildings painted in shades of white, yellow, and red. Wrought-iron balconies gave the streets texture; the many flowers hanging off of them, an extra burst of color. The soft scent of citrus wafted everywhere. Lana breathed in deeply, reveling in the scent.

She was enjoying the walk so much, she almost missed seeing Becky and Nick take a left onto a side street. She hurried to catch up.

When Lana came closer, she heard Becky say to her husband, "What if his agent does find a loophole? Could he impede our deal? We can't let him ruin this for us! We are on the precipice of something great."

Nick took his wife's hands. "Chet will not destroy this opportunity for us. I will make certain he does not, don't you worry." He pulled Becky in for a kiss, but released her quickly when he noticed Lana.

"Hey there," he said easily, "great of you to join us. What did you think about being on the panel?"

Lana blushed, knowing she had been caught eavesdropping. To her relief, neither Nick or Becky seemed to care.

"It was a wonderful learning experience. I especially admire how you and Becky responded to all those comments and questions so quickly and with so much detail. You are both so natural at it."

The travel-blogging couple chuckled. "It comes with experience. We weren't so suave the first few times we were invited to speak in front of a crowd. Nick stuttered so much the public could barely understand him." Becky burst out giggling at the memory.

"It was the nerves," Nick said, showing no sign that he was embarrassed by his wife's comments. "Becky tended to titter her way through most of her answers."

Becky nodded. "It's true. I have this annoying tendency to laugh when I get nervous or scared. I can't control it, either, which is really frustrating sometimes."

"It's too bad you didn't get asked any questions tonight, Lana," Nick said, steering the conversation back to the evening's panel discussion. "It would have been good practice for you."

"Maybe it was better this way," Becky said. "The points you did make during our initial discussion, you did with style and grace. And now you know how these kinds of discussions and Q&A sessions work, so the next time you will be even more prepared."

"Thanks." Lana blushed at the compliment from her social media hero. Becky could find the silver lining in any cloud, it seemed. "I do hope my presence on the panel will help bring my blog more exposure."

"That's why we take part in these, too," Becky agreed. "Presenting or speaking during an international trade show usually does help tremendously, and this one perhaps more than most. Because they were presenting Chet with that lifetime achievement award, the organization promoted the panel discussion more than usual. It's too bad that Chet chose to be so negative. He really should stick with print—he has no sense for being on camera. But I think his deluge of nasty comments only made him look like an out-of-touch, grumpy old man," Becky said.

"He really did make himself look like the fool, not us," Nick agreed.

"You two were incredibly relaxed with those reporters after the discussion ended. And you even turned the conversation around so it was about your blog and videos, instead of Chet's negativity. That was quite a feat!" Lana exclaimed.

"That's sweet." Becky spun around and hugged Lana. She draped an arm over her shoulder and said, "If I can give you one tip, for the next time you are interviewed..."

Becky's voice trailed off as she looked to Lana.

Lana froze, thrilled the successful blogger wanted to share any advice with her. "Yes, please do."

"Mention your website's name as often as possible—in a natural way, of course. It's the best way for potential readers to remember you. *Travel Time* is a catchy name; you should be fine as long as you keep pushing your brand."

Lana nodded in agreement, realizing that all of the panelists had made a point of referring often to their websites and mentioning their product names during the discussion.

"How long did it take for your blog to catch on?" Lana asked.

Becky's pace slowed slightly. "Gosh, we've been posting videos about our travels for five years now, but our subscription channel didn't really take off until we were voted the world's best travel bloggers. Until that happened, Nick and I worked corporate jobs. But once our numbers of subscribers shot up, the advertising began bringing in more than our day jobs did, and we decided to quit and make our hobby our career. It was scary to give up the security of working for someone else, but it ended up being the best decision we have ever made. Now we have total creative freedom and a great reason to travel the world."

"I was thinking of creating videos for my *Travel Time* blog," Lana said tentatively, almost embarrassed to discuss her idea with these successful vloggers. "I sat in on the 'Introduction to Vlogging' workshop at the conference and was shocked by how much the equipment and editing costs. It seems pretty expensive to get started."

"You are right about that, Lana. Without our savings, I doubt we would have taken the leap," Nick explained.

"It is an investment, that is for certain. And not everyone is in the same position we were," Becky admitted. "We both had successful careers and never had time for a vacation. That nest egg we had inadvertently built up was how we were able to finance our initial expenditures. You know that old adage—you have to spend money to make money? It is certainly true in the world of social media advertising."

"Do you really film everything yourselves?" Lana dared to ask. After taking that workshop, she had rewatched a few of their videos. Looking at them with more informed eyes, she was fairly certain that they often used multiple cameras to film certain shots. Though the vloggers didn't specifically claim to do everything themselves, no camerapersons were credited at the end of their videos, nor an editing team.

Becky giggled. "I'll tell you the truth as long, as you promise not to blog about it."

Lana nodded solemnly.

"We did start out filming everything ourselves, but were not really satisfied with the results because our equipment wasn't of a high enough quality," Becky explained. "To make matters worse, we got into trouble with the authorities in several countries because we had not acquired the correct filming permits."

"We ended up paying thousands in bribes to get our gear back," Nick recalled.

Becky nodded. "We got fed up with all the hassles and started hiring local camera crews to film most of the footage. Usually we make extensive shot lists and let the professionals deal with getting the right permits to film them all. We do shoot closeups of each other and some of the narration with our smartphones, but never with our expensive camera gear. That way, the authorities leave us alone because they think we are just regular tourists. The same goes with the editing. We used to do it all ourselves, but a professional editor made it look so much better."

"The results ultimately justified the expense. Our number of subscribers increased substantially after we began using professionals, instead of doing it all ourselves," Nick added.

Lana nodded, taking in all they had to say. How incredible it was of the pair to be so candid with her. They truly were one of the friendliest and down-to-earth couples she had ever met.

Talking about their videos gave Lana the courage to ask them about Chet's cryptic comments. "It sounds like you two do have a television program lined up. Is Chet somehow involved with it?"

Becky's pace slowed. "What do you mean?"

"When Chet made those strange comments during the discussion about presenting a television show, I couldn't help but notice that you two seemed rather shocked." When Lana saw the stricken expression on Becky's face, she added, "Don't worry, I wasn't planning on blogging about it. His comments piqued my curiosity, that's all."

Nick looked uncomfortable, but Becky shrugged her shoulders. "Why can't we tell her the truth? The show is ours."

"It is a painful situation, at least for Chet. A production company had a great idea for a new travel show and asked Chet to present it. But the test shots were so bad that the network's boss rejected it. They didn't want to scrap the show so they went looking for someone else to present it. A few weeks ago, they asked us!" Becky's enthusiasm was infectious.

"Wow, what a wonderful opportunity!" Lana exclaimed.

"It really is. But Chet was not pleased to be dismissed, as you can imagine. He's been making our lives as sour as possible ever since. But after the television network makes the official announcement, he can't do anything else to mess up the deal," Becky rushed to add. "Not that he could have, anyway. We already signed all the paperwork."

"When is it being announced?" Lana asked.

Becky beamed. "Next week. After the tour ends, we are flying out to Los Angeles to take part in the press conference. I can't wait to see what the media's reaction will be. I suspect our number of followers and subscribers is going to skyrocket!"

19

Dinner and Dancing

"Hey, ladies, look at that." Nick stood on the street corner, staring up. The sky was turning shades of pink and purple, and the last rays of sunlight caused the buildings surrounding them to momentarily glow. Tall palm trees swayed in the wind, almost as if they were wishing the sun goodnight.

Lana had been so focused on her conversation with Becky that she was completely unaware of her surroundings. The three stood shoulder to shoulder, silently taking in the glorious view until the hoots and hollers of passing partygoers broke the magical spell.

Their short walk had taken them from the outskirts of the city to a more touristy neighborhood known for its tapas bars and flamenco performances. Lana was shocked to see how busy the streets were. Considering Holy Week had yet to begin, she had not expected to see so many tourists in town already. Yet other guides had warned her that Semana Santa was one of the most popular times to visit the city, drawing close to a million tourists and pilgrims from all over the globe. Based on the number of languages she heard passing her by, they had not been exaggerating.

Nick checked the map on his phone. "The theater should be on our right."

"Good thing you know where to look; the street is practically hidden!" Becky exclaimed as they eyed the tiny passage between buildings. It was more of an alleyway than a street, so narrow that Lana doubted a car could pass through without getting stuck. A neon sign spelling out "Theater Moreno" hung from one of the buildings.

"That's the place," he said.

Lana pushed the door open, unsure what to expect. The grand old hall before them was a pleasant surprise. The interior seemed to be made out of highly polished mahogany wood and lots of red velvet.

Moorish lamps, punctured by a multitude of tiny holes, cast intricate patterns of light across the small hall. Instead of rows of folding seats, round tables encircled by plush chairs dotted the floor. Almost all of the seats were filled, and most of the participants were already sipping a drink.

Lana noted three empty seats and began to walk towards them when a middle-aged dancer approached them. The dark-haired beauty looked familiar. Lana took in her tight polka dot dress, lacy shawl, and the gorgeous fanlike comb in her hair, but she still couldn't place the woman.

"Hello and welcome to Theater Moreno. I am Josepha, one of the principal dancers. Please let me show you to your seats. You are the last to arrive; the show will begin momentarily."

It was the woman who fled the panel discussion after upsetting Chet, Lana realized. During the Q&A, she had been wearing a simple blouse and jeans. Her makeup was now quite theatrical, as was her dress, which is why Lana didn't recognize her straight away. But that lush voice and delightful accent were impossible to hide. *What was it that she asked again, that upset Chet so?* Lana wondered. Before she could recall, they were at their table, directly in front of the raised podium running the breadth of the hall.

Seated around the table were the other members of the discussion panel, with the exception of Chet. He was seated at a smaller fold-out table placed to the far right of the podium, a single glass and half-empty pitcher of sangria on his table.

"What happened? Why is Chet sitting alone?" Lana leaned over and asked Josepha, who kept her back to the travel writer.

The Spanish woman grinned. "My hostess said he was the first to arrive and he immediately demanded a table for one," she whispered back, then added loudly, "We hope you enjoy the performance and dinner."

Lana glanced over at Chet as she took her place, not wanting to make eye contact, when she realized that he was keeping his eyes firmly focused on the empty stage. Despite his bravado, perhaps he was offended that no one wanted to ride over with him, especially in light of his poor performance during the panel discussion, she surmised. Not that he could have expected any other reaction—he had brought it upon himself by being so rude.

Randy and Dwight were seated at a table to their left, with four other speakers from the conference that Lana vaguely recognized. She waved to them and started to rise to say hello when the lights dimmed and the curtain went up.

Standing in the center of the stage was Josepha and a male dancer, frozen in a dramatic pose. Another spotlight illuminated a male singer and guitarist, seated on the left.

Knowing they were about to learn to dance the same steps, Lana kept her eyes glued to Josepha's feet. However, she quickly realized it wasn't just the steps she needed to worry about. The choreographed movements seemed to involve the entire body and were clearly timed to the driving music.

Lana soon gave up, choosing instead to enjoy the performance. Both dancers were incredibly graceful as they strutted and stomped their way across the stage. Though she had enjoyed the flamenco performance at the travel conference, this one was infinitely better. The audience was quickly swept up in the dynamic performance and were clapping along in time with the guitar.

After the second song ended and the tremendous applause died down, the house lights came back on.

"Thank you," Josepha crooned into a microphone. "Our waiters will now bring around a selection of tapas for you to enjoy. In a few minutes, we will continue dancing for you. Let our performance inspire you during the workshop, which will begin after your scrumptious meal."

A team of waiters rapidly served the audience, fifty-strong, from Lana's quick assessment. The podium was quite broad, but not very deep. She wondered where exactly all of them would be dancing soon, or if they going to be attending the workshop in shifts.

As soon as their table was filled with tiny dishes of various meats, cheeses, and vegetables, the lights dimmed again. This time, two guitarists took center stage. After a finger-flying serenade that had all of them clapping enthusiastically, a male singer and two couples joined the musicians on stage. The singer sat between the two guitarists while the dancers took their places in two circles of light. As soon as the singer's voice filled the hall, the two pairs began clapping their hands in perfect tempo. The dancers seemed to absorb the rhythm before the women began circling the men, dancing so their ruffly dresses shimmied and shook in the lights. Their graceful, yet severe, movements paired perfectly with the expressive music.

Lana ate more than her fair share of the tapas, she suspected. But it was so wonderful to be getting the royal treatment, and the food was so delectable it was hard to resist trying just one more bite.

After the entertainers had taken their final bows, Nick leaned over to his wife. "I don't know if we will be as graceful as the professionals, but I can't wait to give it a go."

Lana thought the same. She definitely would not be able to mimic their moves, but it was going to be fun to try.

After the lights came back on, Josepha returned to the podium.

"What did you think?" she asked the public as the lights turned to shine onto them. A loud applause followed. A wicked smile crept over Josepha's face. "Now it is your turn to try. Let us see if any of you can rival our dancers' style and grace."

"Our instructors will now come to your tables to divide you into smaller groups. While you are changing into the traditional clothing of a flamenco dancer, our waiters will clear the floor so we can spread out to better give you hands-on instruction."

She clapped her hands together with a snap. "*¡Buena suerte!* Good luck!"

20

Dressing the Part

A tiny young woman dressed in a ruffly dress made her way over to Lana's table. "I am happy to be your instructor this evening. Flamenco is a dance that not many can master in such a short amount of time. I look forward to seeing which one of you has Spanish blood flowing in their veins."

She crooked her finger, causing those seated to rise. "Before we can dance, we must dress appropriately."

She began to walk towards a staircase leading up and onto the high podium, when she suddenly stopped and walked over to Chet, still seated at his table for one. "You are also part of my group." She smiled encouragingly, but Chet stayed put.

The young dancer held out her hand. "Please, it would be my pleasure to share the flamenco with you. Besides, this evening was organized in your honor. It would be a shame for you to miss out on the best part."

The flattery seemed to work. Chet rose and took her hand, allowing her to lead him up the staircase.

Lana's eyebrows shot up. What did she mean, this evening was organized in his honor? Her hackles were well and truly up, until she realized the woman must have meant that the evening was organized in honor of the conference panelists—not just Chet. The irritation washed away as she followed their guide up to the podium and through a long hallway leading towards an enclosed space behind the stage.

The hall was already filled with panelists from the travel conference, happily chatting as they slowly made their way towards the dressing room at the back. Lana was surprised to see how slowly the line was moving; she figured since dressing up was part of the workshop, things would have gone more quickly.

A few minutes later, the first participants emerged from the dressing room, giggling as they showed off their traditional flamenco costumes. Lana was in awe of the transformation. The women looked so pretty in their dresses and the men so handsome in their suits. Lana couldn't wait to see what she would get to wear. A few minutes later, the hallway became a two-lane passageway of those clothed and ready to dance, and those who were still waiting to enter the dressing space.

When they were halfway through the hallway, the lights suddenly went out and the space was plunged into darkness.

"What's going on?" someone called out.

"Nick—is that your hand on my backside?" Becky asked, her voice filled with anxiety.

"Yes, doll. Sorry, I thought it was your hip," her husband said.

"Someone must have brushed up against the light switch," their young instructor called out. "There are switches next to both doorways. Can someone please turn the lights back on?"

Seconds later, the bulbs flickered back on, filling the space with light and Lana with a sense of relief.

"Wow, it was really dark in here. I couldn't see my hand in front of my face," Becky said, holding her husband tight.

"It is because all of the windows in the building have been blacked out, to ensure no extra light shines onto the podium during our daytime performances. The sunlight ruins the effect of our lighting system," their instructor explained.

Moments later, their group was standing in front of the dressing room door. They were the last to get changed, and Lana was momentarily concerned that there might not be enough clothes left for all of them.

She needn't have worried. The enormous space was chock full of racks, all overflowing with costumes for men and women. On the left were white shirts, black pants, and short black jackets. Lana assumed those were for the male dancers. She gravitated towards the right, where racks full of ruffled dresses, knitted shawls, and lots of lacy fans lined the wall.

A plump woman with salt-and-pepper hair clicked her tongue against her teeth as their group entered the space. "So many tourists today," she muttered in Spanish.

Thanks to classes taken during high school, Lana understood her, but couldn't recall how to respond properly in Spanish. "Oh, is this a larger group than normal?" she asked.

"Yes, it is," the woman responded in English, apparently unfazed that Lana had heard her complaining. "Our maximum is usually two groups of ten at one time. To accommodate the conference's request, they called in more instructors." The woman's face turned sour. "It's too bad they didn't think to bring in another wardrobe person."

The Spanish woman raised her voice, addressing the crowd. "Ladies, which dress would you like?" She pointed towards the racks. "The sizes are on the hangers. Be warned, the dresses are rather tight in the waist. We also have skirts with elastic waistbands, if you prefer. Changing rooms are along the back wall."

She then stepped over to the men and began handing out pants and jackets, before pointing at the shoe selection.

After getting the men clothed, the Spanish woman returned to the ladies. Serena, Amber, and Becky were already trying on various ruffled dresses, but Lana's hand wavered over two frocks, unsure which one would suit her better. Noticing her indecision, the dresser grabbed a completely different one and shoved it in Lana's hands.

"This should fit you perfectly."

Lana's eyes widened; no one had ever sized her up with their eyes before. Full of skepticism, she crossed to a changing room and stepped into the dress, expecting it to be far too large or small. It fit as if it was made for her. Not only that, it was gorgeous, and the cut made her look even skinnier than she truly was.

Lana threw back the curtain. "I love it! Thank you. How did you size me up like that?"

The woman smiled and shrugged. "It comes with the job and lots of experience."

Lana smoothed down the polka-dotted fabric, reveling in the softness of it.

The Spanish woman eyed her critically, then nodded. "It suits you quite well."

She then turned to an open drawer full of hairpins of various sizes. While Lana had been getting dressed, the Spanish woman had helped the rest of her group choose decorations for their hair as well as a pair of thick-heeled shoes. Lana took in the broad selection of hair combs, tiaras, and flower-encrusted headbands. She couldn't wait to see what the woman chose for her.

The dresser's fingers hovered over a rather small comb, before she finally plucked up the largest of the bunch. Lana drew in her breath as she eyed the magnificent creation before her. The comb was as large as her hand and seemed to be carved from one piece of tortoiseshell. Much of the shell had been chipped away, leaving an intricate, lace-like pattern. She almost dared not to touch it, it seemed so delicate.

"You have enough hair to wear this *peinetas*," the woman said resolutely.

Lana fingered her locks, now slightly longer than her shoulder blades, and blushed. She had been letting her hair grow for the past year and was happy with how it was turning out. After years of having a short bob, she was surprised to see the long look suited her.

"Is that real tortoiseshell? It is so beautiful. What if I break it?" Lana said, marveling at the craftmanship and the marbly texture.

With a secretive smile, the dresser bashed the comb against the countertop. Lana's heart about stood still. How could she destroy something so beautiful? Yet the clip didn't break, but bent with the blow instead.

"The cheap, plastic combs you find in souvenir shops are as fragile as porcelain, which makes them useless for workshops such as these. But these old-fashioned ones are almost impossible to break. My grandfather had a shop full of these things when the tortoise was declared an endangered species. Since we can't sell them, we should have enough combs to last us for many years to come."

When the costume designer handed her the comb, Lana held it up to the light, admiring the form and size. Attached to the back were three thin metal needles almost as long as her forearm. She touched her fingertip to the end of one and felt a prick.

"Be careful, the pins don't bend and are incredibly sharp. They have to be, otherwise they won't slide easily through the hair."

The woman grabbed Lana's hair and twisted it into a bun before she could protest. She then pulled the *peinetas* out of Lana's hand and shoved it into her hair before spinning her around so she was facing a mirror. "You look ravishing. Now go dance!"

Becky, Serena, and Amber had been watching the scene unfold as they waited for Lana to finish. All were clearly intrigued by the beautiful comb.

"Do you have another one of those?" Becky asked. "It's gorgeous."

"I'm afraid it won't work with your hair. It's too short—there is nothing to stick the pins through."

Becky frowned and ran her hand through her short bob. "Oh, yeah, it is too short for a comb now. And those pins do look quite sharp. I wouldn't want to have one of those rubbing against my neck when we are dancing."

"You most certainly would not—it would break the skin. And we don't want you lovely ladies bleeding all over our dresses," the dresser teased.

Serena also seemed to be enthralled with the tortoiseshell comb. "No, you most certainly would not. But my hair is quite long. It should work." Serena began to pull the tiara-like headdress out of her hair when the dresser clicked her tongue again.

"Ladies, you are the last group to dress. If you don't get started soon, you won't have time to learn the most basic steps. Now go and dance the flamenco!"

21

Magic Time

Lana swished down the hallway towards the podium, feeling quite sexy in her frilly dress. *Too bad Alex couldn't be here to see me in it*, she thought, promising herself to ask someone to take her picture for him.

When she stepped onto the podium, she realized that she was the last to arrive. The discussion panel participants were standing on the left. Randy, Dwight, and the other participants who had been sitting at their table were on the right. Down on the main floor where they had eaten, four groups were already busy learning their first steps.

After she joined her group, Josepha clapped sharply, attracting their attention once again. The Spanish dancer stood on the edge of the podium, clearly addressing all of the workshop participants.

"Flamenco is more than a dance. It is, for many, a way of life. Explore your emotions—love, loss, anger, sadness, and joy—when you dance these steps. Keep them in your mind and heart as you move, and your body will respond better to the rhythm and instructions."

"Josepha?" Chet exclaimed. "I hardly recognized you in that getup. You're a much better dancer than hotelier. I guess I did you a favor." His belly laugh resounded around the podium.

Josepha's eyes flashed but, she ignored his insult and turned, instead, to the two instructors standing on the podium. "Let us begin."

If looks could kill, Lana thought.

The young dancer leading Lana's group cleared her throat to get their attention. "Welcome. Today my partner and I will demonstrate a few basic dance steps before helping you to mimic them. We will start with a simple hand-foot exercise."

She and the male instructor leading Randy's group began clapping their hands and stomping their feet in a seemingly simple rhythm. Lana kept her focus on the female instructor, silently memorizing her movements. The woman lifted her arms up in the air and pushed her elbows away from her body in a sharp angle as she raised her knee before stomping her foot hard onto the wooden floor. Lana now understood why they were wearing these clunky shoes; the thick heels were necessary to re-create the stomping noise.

The two dancers then began to slowly circle each other while clapping and stomping, keeping their eyes locked as they moved. Lana held her arms up and pushed her elbows out, hoping to at least get part of the dance step right.

After they finished demonstrating the seemingly simple technique, they looked to their students and smiled. "Now it's your turn," the female dancer said. She nodded to Becky and Nick, and then Ted and Erica. "You are obviously already paired up." She gestured towards Amber. "Miss, why don't you dance with this gentleman?"

When the instructor pointed to Chet, the travel writer balked. "I am not dancing with anyone in this group. I demand to be put in a different one, otherwise I am submitting a complaint to the organization."

"After all the horrible things you said about us, we aren't exactly looking forward to dancing with you either," Nick snapped at Chet.

Josepha strode over from the back of the podium the second Chet opened his mouth. She laid a hand on the young instructor's shoulder before saying in Spanish, "Let me deal with this one."

"Alright, why don't you move over there." Josepha waved towards Randy's group, then pointed to Dwight. "You, sir. Would you switch places with this gentleman?"

"Sure," Dwight said and raced over to stand next to Serena.

The lifestyle blogger took a step away from him. "I want to dance with Amber," Serena said before grabbing the environmentalist by the wrist and twirling her around.

"It would be my honor," Amber replied.

Dwight's expression darkened. *Is he in love with Serena?* Lana wondered. He did seem to want to be close to her. Lana wouldn't be surprised—the young blogger was gorgeous and successful. But, aside from her fleeting interest in him during the second day of the travel conference, Serena pretty much ignored him. To Lana, that meant she was not interested in him, but Dwight was apparently not getting the hint. Although Lana didn't blame the young woman for not wanting to dance with Dwight for fear of leading him on, she wasn't looking forward to taking the bullet for her guest. *I bet he has two left feet*, Lana thought as he stood before her and bowed slightly.

Unfortunately for Lana, she was right. When dancing the flamenco, men and women did not hold hands, but did execute choreographed moves that brought their bodies dangerously close to each other without actually touching. At least, that's how the professionals did it.

Dwight and Lana stumbled and jerked around, instead of drifting gracefully. In no time, Lana's feet were covered with bruises. Neither one of them could get the rhythm right, and both were stepping on each other's toes more than the dance floor. It only got worse as the dance passes became more complex. The instructors were incredibly patient with them, but there really wasn't enough time to master any moves—only to get acquainted with them.

"Let your inhibitions go and feel the passion moving your limbs. Relax into your poses and most of all—enjoy yourself!" their young instructor said between reminders to keep their hips forward, chin up, chest open, shoulder blades back, knees high, and elbows out.

Lana wished she could do any of the above. She was having trouble mastering the most basic movements and was rather embarrassed by her lack of rhythm. As she pulled up her knee and stomped her heel, Lana felt like a buffalo stumbling around the floor.

Ted and Erica were faring much better, but were still not graceful. However, Nick and Becky were sashaying their way around the floor as if they had been taking lessons for years. Lana wondered whether there was anything the couple did not excel at.

Josepha also noticed how well they were dancing. "Where did you learn to dance so beautifully?"

"We took a two-day class in Argentina, and I guess it stuck with us," Becky laughed. "We filmed much of our experience and posted about it on our site. It's one of our most popular videos of 2019. We would love to know what you think of it in the comments," Becky said as she stuck her hand into her purse, whipped out a business card, and handed it to the woman before she could react.

Lana was impressed. Becky was truly prepared for every moment.

Becky's remark about their video made Lana think about her own blog. This class would make a great blog post, even if it was only photos and text. She would have to watch Becky and Nick's video as inspiration.

I should have taken photos of the professional dancers and our dinner, she chastised herself as she pulled out her phone and snapped a selfie, and then a few of the two groups practicing.

After they had a few minutes to practice, their young instructor began to clap. "Excellent work, everyone! Now it is time to try a *pasada*, or passing step. You will use this to change places with your partner on the dance floor." The two instructors illustrated the technique before the two groups attempted to mimic them.

The longer they danced, the more chaotic the evening became. Each new dance pass required increasingly more space, which meant the two groups on the podium began bumping into each other.

Chet couldn't seem to let an opportunity to make a snide observation slide, and grew increasingly critical of the dancers' instructions, as well as his fellow participants' movements.

Lana noticed Becky and Nick looking towards Chet, then whispering to each other between practicing the dance steps. Amber and Serena also seemed to be keeping an eye on the travel writer. Only Ted and Erica appeared to be ignoring him completely.

When Chet began berating his instructor for not explaining a movement better, Lana noticed Josepha moving closer to his group.

"This workshop is simply a short introduction to the basic steps. We don't have time to teach you how to dance the flamenco in an hour," Josepha said, in her instructor's defense.

When she intervened, Chet turned on her again. "I just realized your last name is Moreno, like the theater. Is this your family's business? If I had known it was, I would not have recommended it in my guidebooks. I guess it is time to post another update." He laughed manically, and Josepha's eyes narrowed to slits. Yet she said nothing in return.

Lana was amazed that the Spanish dancer could turn the other cheek, until she saw Josepha's foot shoot out right as Chet danced past her.

He fell hard, bashing his nose into the wooden floor. When he rose, Lana noticed a few specks of blood on his bowtie.

"What is wrong with you?" Chet raged as he dabbed his bleeding nose with a cloth handkerchief.

"Watch where you are dancing," Josepha admonished.

Josepha's action seemed to have been noticed by all and interpreted as a green light to do the same. Becky soon made a wide pass around her husband, her extended elbows jabbing into Chet's back.

"Watch out!" she chastised when Chet turned to glare at her.

Serena also took a swing, literally, when she whipped her hair into Chet's face.

After the third embarrassment, Chet stood still on the podium and stomped his feet like an angry toddler. "That is enough! You are not going to ruin my evening. I am the man of the hour, after all."

"We are all VIPs tonight, Chet," Nick said.

Chet puffed up his chest. "I'm the one who received a lifetime achievement award—not you two wannabes."

"A lifetime achievement award is an acknowledgment of what you have done, not what you will do. It says nothing about your future," Becky retorted.

"Your show has not yet been recorded, correct? Until they say 'action,' anything can happen."

"If your performance was so great, why did the producers call us?"

Chet's enormous smile dimmed, and his fists balled up. "How dare you speak to me like that!" His aggressive tone caused the rest to turn and stare.

The female instructor stepped in between them. "Please—we are here to dance, not fight. Harness that emotion and use it to fuel your steps; let it move your hips, shoulders, and arms!"

"We'll soon see whose show makes it to air," Chet growled before moving back to his group.

The female instructor whirled around to her male counterpart. "Let us continue with the *careos*, or passing waltzing step."

22

Dancing the Flamenco

After Lana's group had learned their sixth dance step, Chet's group was still practicing the fifth move. Chet was pushing the instructor again, as he had done the entire hour. His demands that they receive more guidance were slowing them all down. The poor instructor seemed to be getting more and more agitated with both Chet's need for perfectionism, as well as his insistence that they be given a chance to practice all six moves—as the other groups had done.

Lana glanced discreetly at her watch. It was already 11 p.m. Would they allow Chet's group to finish before wrapping up the workshop? Her feet were throbbing from the too-tight heels and many bruises she had sustained while practicing with Dwight.

Lana was so grateful when her instructor clapped twice, signaling for them to stop practicing. "We hope you enjoyed your introduction to the flamenco. You were all great—give yourself a round of applause!"

Josepha also joined in, smiling at the small group as she clapped and walked over to their instructor.

Lana wiped the sweat from her forehead as discreetly as she could, then took a look at the other dancers in her group. Dwight was already vying for Serena's attention again, but the young blogger was completely unaware of his existence. Instead, she had her phone out and was showing Amber something on the screen. Whatever it was brought a smile to both of their faces.

Ted and Erica were standing with their arms around each other's waists. Becky and Nick were still dancing, glowing with happiness as they blew kisses to each other. *They are really in love*, Lana thought.

"What do we do now?" Dwight asked.

When Josepha and their instructor looked to the hallway, Lana followed their gaze. The four groups on the floor had finished before the two on the podium and the participants were slowly snaking their way towards the dressing room. Lana suspected that changing back into their normal clothes would take more time than getting dressed up in their flamenco costumes did.

"Why don't we wait a moment for things to quiet down. It seems we all ended at the same time," the young dancer said.

Dwight frowned. "Having so many groups practicing at once doesn't seem like a smart way of running things."

The young woman cringed, then replied in a defensive tone, "We usually don't give lessons to so many participants at the same time, but we made an exception for the travel expo. That's why we had groups dancing on the floor, as well."

Josepha added loudly, "While we are waiting, why don't we practice the last *pasada* one more time?"

Dwight turned to Lana and assumed the initial stance. She groaned internally as their instructor began clapping her hands in a steady rhythm, setting their tempo. After several bumbling passes and near misses, Lana noted the hallway was less busy. Several participants had already changed and were exiting the theater, meaning there should now be enough room for their group. With a little luck, they could be changed and out of the theater before Chet's group had finished. From the looks of things, his group was going to be practicing a while longer.

After Dwight stepped on her foot for a fifth time, Lana stopped dancing. "Gosh, I am all pooped out. Do you mind if we call it a night?" she said loudly, hoping their instructor would hear her.

Josepha looked to the hallway again. "It looks like you have free passage to the changing area. Thank you for a lovely evening. I hope you enjoyed dancing the flamenco!"

Lana sighed in relief. Before their group could enter the hallway, Josepha walked over to Chet's group and clapped for their attention. "It is wonderful to see how much you are all enjoying your experience, but it is time to wrap up the workshops for the night."

"But we haven't learned the last dance step yet!" Chet exclaimed.

"Let's go, people," Lana mumbled, mentally willing her group to pick up the pace so they could get in and out before the other group made it to the changing room. Chet had been making horrible comments all evening, and Lana figured he would continue to do so, given the chance. The man was getting on her last nerve and she was afraid she would not be able to keep quiet if he did.

But her group was not rushing towards the changing room. Instead, they seemed to be dragging their feet. Lana stood up on her toes to see who was at the front. It was Becky and Nick, deep in conversation and seemingly oblivious to the rest. When Becky stopped just inside of the hallway, Serena and Amber both bumped into the couple. The young bloggers were so focused on their phones, they had apparently not been paying attention to their classmates' movements.

"Sorry for the holdup," Becky said. "I must have lost the clip that was holding this headband in place."

She squeezed past the two bloggers, around Dwight, and then Ted and Erica, to return to the podium. Lana, who was still at the back, joined in the search, scanning the floor as they slowly walked across the floor. Seconds later, she noticed a small glimmer of metal in the spotlights. "Here it is!" she called out, triumphantly returning the hair clip to Becky.

Becky bowed deeply. "I owe you one. I don't know if they would have made me pay for it, otherwise."

"I suppose we could have declared it as an incidental expense," Nick noted, as he leaned against the hallway.

"Still, now we don't have to worry about their reaction." Becky replied as she fastened the clip into place. "Does this look right?" she asked Lana.

Lana eyed the headband critically and began to straighten it out, until she realized they were about to take off their costumes. It didn't really matter if the fake flower attached to it was slightly off-center. "It's fine," she replied cheerily.

"Say, does anyone want to grab a sangria after this?" Nick asked the group.

"That sounds like a great idea. It's still early, and Seville's supposed to have a great bar scene," Dwight enthused.

Early? Lana thought, wondering what Dwight would consider to be late. *Maybe I am just getting old,* she considered. After such a long and intense day, she was really looking forward to having a nightcap with Randy before crawling into her bathtub for a long soak. She had discovered muscles that she didn't know that she had during their dance workshop. Most of all, her feet were really killing her.

"I'm game," Amber called out.

"Sounds good," Serena agreed.

Meanwhile, Chet's group, after his initial protest was overruled by Josepha, also began shuffling towards the hallway. Chet, of course, tried charging to the front of the line. "What's the holdup?" he called out from behind Lana and Becky.

So much for avoiding Chet, she thought.

Instead of snapping at the irritating man, Lana knelt down to rub at her foot before deciding to take off the clunky heels instead. She'd gotten the first strap open when Chet groused, "Would you get a move on? I want to change my clothes."

Lana had had enough. She twisted around from her squatted position to give him a piece of her mind, when the space was plunged into darkness.

"Not again," a male voice groaned. Was that Dwight? *It is strange how people sound different in the pitch black,* she thought.

"If someone would be so kind as to turn on the lights," Josepha said.

There was a scuffling noise as people moved around the hallway, presumably trying to find the light switch. Figuring the problem would soon be resolved, Lana felt for the second buckle, when someone pulled roughly on her hair.

"Ow!" she yelped, her hand automatically going to her scalp. It felt as if several strands had been torn out.

A gurgling noise startled her, just as someone or something whipped past her, knocking her off balance. Lana fell backwards onto something soft, just as the lights came back on.

Lana's scalp really hurt. She looked at her palm expecting to see blood, but there was none, only a few more loose hairs. She turned to see what she may have caught her hair on, when she noticed what she had landed on.

"No!" Lana's scream made everyone turn. Underneath her was Chet Rogers. The travel writer's perpetually smug expression had finally been replaced with another emotion—that of astonishment. Lana sprung up and off of him, but the travel writer didn't respond. Instead, the trickle of blood seeping from his neck grew into a river. Its source was three needle-like pins, topped by a tortoiseshell comb.

"Is that a *peinetas* sticking out of his neck?" Amber asked.

"What happened?" Josepha cried as she pushed through the small crowd now encircling Chet. When she saw the body and pool of blood, the Spanish dancer threw her hand over her mouth. *"¡Dios mío!"*

23

Not Again

"This can't be happening again!" Lana screamed. Was she an angel of death or a magnet for murderers? Why did so many people die during her tours?

The hallway filled with screams and cries as Chet's condition registered with all those present. Becky gasped as Nick turned away. Erica buried her face in Ted's chest. Serena's hands flew to the sides of her cheeks, Dwight's mouth dropped open, and Amber's eyes welled up with tears.

Several theater employees rushed towards the stage, stopping short of actually climbing up onto the podium.

The rest stepped closer to the body, slowly encircling his lifeless corpse.

"Is he really dead?" Becky whispered to Nick.

"Looks like it," he said and held his wife close.

The blood spurting out of Chet's neck had slowed to a trickle. Lana didn't need to be a doctor to know that he was gone.

Randy, however, stepped forward and checked his wrist for a pulse before shaking his head.

"He can't be dead!" Dwight cried as he bent down to get a closer look at Chet.

Lana, too, felt like shedding a tear. Seeing a life taken was a traumatic experience, even if the victim was not a beloved human being. *Maybe Dwight does have a sensitive side*, she thought.

Until he added, "Darn it! I needed him alive, to win that lawsuit. He's no good to me dead."

He stomped away to the side of the podium, throwing his arms over his torso as he sulked like a child sent to the corner for a timeout.

"What do we do now?" Amber asked.

"Call the police," Randy responded. He reached into his pocket. "Shoot, my phone is in the dressing room."

"I can call them from the office," Josepha said.

"Isn't that Lana's *peinetas?*" Serena asked, her tone the embodiment of innocence.

"What do you mean, my hair comb?" She reached for the tortoiseshell comb in her hair, but felt nothing. Her eyes darted towards the one sticking out of Chet's neck.

"Oh no," Lana mumbled. It did look like the one she had been given to wear. Could this day get any worse? "I didn't hurt him! Right after the lights went out, I felt a tug on my hair. Someone else must have pulled it out of my bun and stabbed him with it."

"I didn't do it!" Amber huffed, then turned to Serena, almost expectantly.

"Don't look at me," Serena snapped. "Why would I want to hurt him? His remarks didn't affect my number of followers."

"We didn't have any reason to harm him, either," Becky and Nick added, almost simultaneously.

"Wasn't he going to mess up your TV deal?" Serena asked.

"He threatened to do so, but he could not have hindered us. We already signed the contract," Nick assured, before adding, "But Chet was going to block Ted's new website."

Ted's eyes widened. "What? No, he was bluffing to get under my skin. That was his *modus operandi*—if he couldn't win, then he did everything he could to devastate those who did."

Everyone's eyes turned back to Lana. "Why would I want to hurt him?" she cried indignantly.

"He was going to destroy your employer's tour company because she used her connections to get you on the discussion panel. If he'd have published it, I bet you would have lost your job."

When Lana opened her mouth to protest, Dwight added, "Don't try and deny it—I heard you tell Randy about Chet's threats yesterday morning. In my book, you had the most to lose." Dwight stared at Lana with a self-righteous expression.

Before she could retort, a soft voice spoke to them from the hallway. "Thank you for enlightening me to all of your motives."

24

Too Many Suspects

A middle-aged man in a three-piece suit emerged from the shadows, accompanied by two men in uniform, the word *"policia"* printed in large letters on the backs of their jackets.

"Police Inspector Diaz," he said. "It is good to make your acquaintance."

"How did you get here so fast?" Dwight demanded.

"I was attending to another matter one block from here when the call came in." Inspector Diaz looked around the space and the people clustered onto the small stage, before taking in the dead body sprawled out on the floor.

"Let us move down to the main floor so the forensics team can get to work."

The officers waved them down the staircase and onto the floor where they had eaten dinner earlier. As soon as they had moved from the podium, a team of persons clad in white ascended the stairs and bent over the crime scene. Lana turned her back to them, unable to watch as they documented Chet's last position in life.

"Señora Moreno tells me the incident happened a few minutes ago. She has filled me in on most of the details. Where were you standing when Señor Rogers was killed?" The inspector's voice was gentle, yet commanding.

Everyone began explaining simultaneously where they had been standing when the lights went out, but their remarks overlapped and jumbled together.

The inspector raised his hands and waved for them to stop. "We aren't getting anywhere this way." He picked up two chairs and placed them on one side of the floor. "Let us pretend this is the entrance to the hallway leading to the changing room. On either side are the light switches. Why don't you all return to where you were standing when the lights went out? Maybe then we can puzzle out who may have accidentally turned them off."

Josepha, Nick, and Becky stood in between the two chairs, as if they had just entered the hallway. Ted and Erica moved so they were behind the vlogging couple. Amber stopped behind them while Dwight and Lana took up the rear. A few feet back from Lana stood Randy and the participants in his group. The space left empty between the two guides was where Chet had been. Both of their instructors stood on the other side of the floor, far away from the hallway.

Serena frowned at the group. "Honestly, I'm not sure where I was standing exactly because I was reading my email."

"You were next to me," Amber said, waving her over. Serena shrugged and joined her friend.

"Wait, I was standing behind Amber and Serena, not in front of them," Dwight said. "I remember because I was looking over their shoulders to see what they were looking at on Serena's phone."

Amber rolled her eyes. "That's creepy."

Ted and Erica looked confused for a moment, until Ted snapped his fingers. "Of course! He's right. I was cuddling with Erica and didn't really notice where we were standing." He smiled at his fiancée before stepping back to make room for Dwight.

After everyone settled into position, Lana looked at her group. "That's not correct," she mumbled. Becky was next to her when the lights went out, wasn't she? Or had she missed seeing Becky return to her husband's side when she bent down to unbuckle her heels? She had been so focused on her feet, she hadn't been keeping track of the others' movements.

Unfortunately for Lana, the policeman heard her. "What is not correct?"

"I thought Becky was at the back with me…" Lana looked to the floor as her voice trailed off. "You know what, I was so focused on my shoes that I can't say for certain where anyone was standing when the lights went off. Pretend I didn't say anything," Lana begged, hoping that Becky wouldn't be upset with Lana for mentioning her name. "It doesn't matter anyway. When the lights came back on, everyone was in a different position."

The officer looked to Becky and raised an eyebrow at her. "Were you at the front or back of the group?"

"I was standing at the front with my husband, but then returned to the podium to look for my missing hairclip, which Lana discovered. After she gave it to me, I went back up to be with Nick." She blushed and looked up at her husband with doe eyes. "Nick had just pulled me in for a kiss. Apparently I'd closed my eyes right when the lights went out because I didn't notice it was dark until someone began screaming."

"Anyone of us could have accidentally brushed up against the light switch when they passed," Amber said.

Nick nodded solemnly. "That's right."

The inspector walked over to Lana and gazed at the empty space behind her. "You were standing directly in front of the victim?"

"Yes," Lana confirmed, afraid to say more for fear that her voice would crack.

He looked to her feet. "What is wrong with your shoes?"

"I was taking them off because they are too small and my feet were killing me."

"So you were bent over, right in front of the victim?"

"I guess. I didn't know Chet was behind me until he started complaining about the line moving too slowly. Before I could turn around, the lights went out."

"And he was stabbed with your *peinetas*?"

"Yes—but anyone could have grabbed it." She held out her hand, still filled with loose hairs. "Someone pulled the comb out of my hair and took a bunch of strands with it. I'm surprised that my scalp isn't bleeding."

"We will fingerprint the *peinetas*, and all of you, of course." He looked at the considerable space between where Chet had been and Randy's group. "Why were you standing so far back from the victim?"

"The guy had been acting like a jerk the entire workshop, and after it finished, he started pushing the others to hurry up. I wasn't in a rush, so I figured it was better to give him some space," Randy said, and the others in his group nodded.

"Hmmm," the inspector murmured before turning his attention to Josepha. In rapid-fire Spanish, he questioned her briefly, but it was clear from her answers that Josepha denied knowing Chet.

Why is she lying? Lana wondered. Josepha and Chet must have known each other, given their cryptic yet personal exchanges during the dance workshop.

But then again, everyone in her group had a reason to want to harm Chet. It could have been anyone up on that podium.

The investigator looked to the conference participants clustered around Randy. The four had been part of his and Chet's workshop group. "How did you know the victim?"

"I saw him speak at the conference, and he seemed pretty awful, to be honest. But I didn't know him well enough to want to harm him!" a middle-aged man said.

"He seemed quite grumpy," another offered. "But I had never met him in person before."

When the inspector returned his sights to Lana and her group, she had to work to keep her expression neutral. "Until we know more about this murder, you are all suspects."

Lana's hackles rose at the man's words. That was a new approach to her—declaring that all were under suspicion. Before she could retort, he continued.

"Yet, I cannot arrest you all. My boss would not allow it."

Lana sighed, feeling slightly relieved.

"However, I can confiscate all of your passports until we have had a chance to check your backgrounds and connections to the victim. My officers will also take your fingerprints so we can compare them with any found on the *peinetas*."

He waited a beat for his words to settle in. After a round of protests, all of the tourists reluctantly handed over their identification. Only the Spanish citizens were exempt.

"But why us? It could have been anyone, right?" Ted asked.

"Because the outer doors were locked to prevent anyone from trying to break in while the workshops were taking place. And because the other participants had already changed back into their own clothes, there was no one else in the hallway. My skills of deduction tell me it must have been one of you."

The group turned on each other, everyone eyeing their neighbor as a potential killer.

25

Married To Her Hotel

April 11—Day Four of the World Travelers Expo in Seville, Spain

Lana's head was swimming. Another murder. At least it wasn't one of her clients that was killed this time. Though her group was being questioned by the police—again.

Scary dreams of knife-wielding dancers and dirty jail cells had haunted her sleep. To spare herself more nightmares, Lana rose earlier than usual and took a long, hot shower, hoping the steamy water would help clear her mind.

Given the circumstances, it was impossible to think of anything but Chet's murder. Seeing as her hair comb was used to killed him, and she was literally on top of his body when the lights went back on, Lana was certain the police considered her a prime suspect. She kept her fingers crossed that someone else's fingerprints would be found on the murder weapon, yet the rational part of her mind told her not to hold her breath. All the murderer would have had to do to hide his or her identity was drag their hand across the comb as they released it, to smudge their prints.

Lana's mind swirled with possibilities—each more far-fetched than the next. Her brain refused to accept that the killer was a member of her tour group. If that were so, she might just break mentally.

Yet if it wasn't one of her guests, who could have done it? The other participants in Randy's group didn't seem to know the travel writer, at least according to the statements they gave the police. And they were all standing a few feet behind Chet. How could they have gotten to the light switch or Lana without anyone having noticed? The two dance instructors were also not close enough to either Chet or the light switches to have done it.

That left Josepha Moreno. She and Chet must have known each other well, given the personal nature of the insults he had flung at her. Josepha had also tried to embarrass Chet at the discussion panel, and Lana was certain the dancer had intentionally tripped him during the flamenco workshop.

She grabbed a notebook and pen before opening her phone's internet browser. Chet had said something about Josepha being a better dancer than hotelier. That was a starting point. When she typed Josepha Moreno's name into a search engine, she was surprised to see many links to the flamenco theater and her performances as a professional dancer, but no recent mentions of a hotel. Only after Lana added "hotel" to her search query did a link on TripAdvisor appear. Josepha had once been the owner of a bed and breakfast in Cordoba, but it had gone bankrupt four years earlier. Lana's brow furrowed as she noted all of the glowing five-star reviews it had received. Why did such a wonderful-sounding hotel close?

Lana clicked on the filter selecting only the one-star reviews. When she read the complaints, her skin began to crawl. Two months before they closed, guests began complaining about unsanitary conditions in the restaurant and hotel rooms, and there were even several mentions of bedbugs and cockroaches.

That's disgusting, but it still doesn't explain Chet's involvement, Lana thought. Only after she refined the search results to include "Only Footprints" did a link appear that clarified Chet's role in the hotel's downfall.

In a long blog post about over-tourism and the effect it can have on popular hotels, Chet asserted that he had witnessed how several renowned establishments skimped on maintenance or their restaurant menu, yet were still charging the same exorbitant prices. Josepha's hotel was Chet's main example and he crucified her B&B in the article, harping on the same unsanitary conditions mentioned in the one-star reviews. *That explained*

Chet's crack about her being a better dancer than hotelier, Lana realized. But could his article really have caused her hotel to go under so quickly? Or did Josepha do it to herself by not maintaining her establishment?

Whatever the reason, Josepha's hotel closed soon after Chet's blog post appeared on the Only Footprints website. Now she was the general manager and a dancer-instructor at the Moreno Theater, a business that had been in her family for the past three generations. From the names on the organizational chart, several of the dancers and waitstaff appeared to be relatives. Would any of them have helped Josepha harm Chet? Lana again considered his position in the middle of the stage. How would someone have jumped up onto the old wooden podium, done the deed, and then sprung back down again, without anyone having heard them?

Lana tapped her pen against her chin, as she considered Josepha's motive and her ability to have committed the murder. She was close to one of the switches when the lights went out. Though how did Josepha manage to get to Lana's comb and stab Chet, then race back to the light switch in a matter of seconds? It seemed impossible, but then again, Josepha was a dancer, and it was her family's theater. She knew the space better than anyone else.

Lana stared at Moreno Theater's website, knowing that she couldn't leave Seville until she had talked to Josepha. It was imperative to find out more about her problems with Chet. Josepha had, after all, lied to the police about her connection to Chet, meaning they probably wouldn't bother to look any deeper.

Her group was leaving early tomorrow morning to see more of Andalucía. Lana clicked on the theater's contact information and noticed that the doors opened at 9:30 and their first class of the day started at 10 a.m. If Josepha wasn't there, she hoped someone would either give her number to Lana or allow her to leave the Spanish lady a note.

The final event of the travel conference, a fancy luncheon and networking session, was scheduled to start at noon. If Randy didn't mind her skipping breakfast, it would be easy enough to go to the theater and be back at the hotel before her group rode over to the conference center.

She looked at her watch, noting that it was already seven in the morning.

Most of her guests would be making their way to the breakfast room around this time. "Better to investigate on a full stomach," she mumbled.

As expected, Randy didn't have any problem with keeping an eye on their group this morning. *I'm going to miss working with him, he is so easygoing,* she thought, hoping that Dotty's new recruits were as relaxed as he was.

When she pushed the door to the Moreno Theater open at 9:30 sharp, Spanish guitar music blared through the speakers. Josepha and two others were moving tables and chairs around, getting ready for the new day. *Life does go on,* Lana mused.

When Josepha noticed Lana hovering around the entrance, she stopped what she was doing and crossed quickly over to her. When she was came closer, Josepha's expression changed from neutral to guarded.

"You took part in our flamenco classes last night. Lana Hansen, correct? What do you want?" Josepha stopped a few feet away and crossed her arms over her torso. Without her extensive makeup on, the dancer looked ten years younger and quite vulnerable.

"For you to tell me the truth," Lana blurted out. Josepha rolled her eyes and began to walk away when Lana pressed, "Josepha, why did you bait Chet at the panel discussion? You said something about him using his blog to ruin honest businesses. Did you mean your bed and breakfast?"

"Why should I talk to you? The police suspect that you are the killer," Josepha scoffed. "It was your comb in his neck, and you were sitting on top of him when the lights went on."

"At least I didn't lie to the police."

Josepha's arms tightened around her torso. "What do you want?"

"You told the police that you didn't know him, but it was clear from his insulting comments that you two were already acquainted. This morning, I read that article about your B&B on Only Footprints' blog. Is that why your hotel went bankrupt? I bet the police will move you higher up their suspect list once they discover that connection. If you don't answer my questions, then I am going to call the inspector." Lana held her gaze as steely as she could.

Josepha blew out her cheeks in exasperation. "I knew it was a bad idea to go to that conference. When I saw he was part of that discussion panel, I couldn't pass up the opportunity to embarrass him in public."

"How did you know him? Was he a regular guest at your bed and breakfast?"

"My hotel was one of the most popular in Cordoba," Josepha said proudly. "That is where we met, when he stayed at my B&B several years ago. We had a short affair, but it was not serious for me. I was happily married to my hotel and had no desire to sell it and travel the world with him."

Josepha must have noticed Lana's expression of disbelief because she hastily added, "He could be quite charming when he wanted to be. But when Chet didn't get what he wanted, he turned into a spiteful monster."

She held her chin up high. "He could not accept that I did not want to be his lover, and he ruined my business as revenge. Soon after his article appeared, several new reviews were posted, all complaining about poor hygiene. No guest had ever complained of bugs in my hotel! Chet must have been behind those bad reviews, but I couldn't prove it."

She threw up her hands, flashing her perfectly manicured fingernails. "Clients started calling to cancel their reservations the day the article appeared, and soon we were empty. I had just spent my savings renovating one of the floors to create more rooms, and the banks refused to extend me any more loans. Chet's article unfairly sullied my business's name when we needed new customers the most! It was impossible to survive financially so I had to sell it at a significant loss." Josepha looked away as she wiped a tear off her cheek.

"Is that why you are working here?"

Josepha's expression darkened. "After everything that had happened, I had no choice but to work for the family business again. I loathe this job—we earn so little and work long hours entertaining irritating tourists. I hated Chet for crushing my dreams."

"Is that why you killed him?" Lana pressed.

"I hated Chet, but I did not kill him. I have had plenty of opportunities to murder him in the past, but did not do so." Josepha smiled mischievously.

"What do you mean?" Lana asked.

"A few months after he posted that horrible article about my hotel, he stayed in my cousin's bed and breakfast in Madrid for a week. When she called to tell me, we joked about poisoning his breakfast, but didn't actually do anything. My cousin did give me the profits from his stay." Her expression grew wistful. "He gave her hotel a glowing five-star review. I wish I'd had a chance to tell him that she was family, just to see the look on his face."

Wow, she is extremely bitter, Lana thought.

"And before you start to think I bided my time and for some reason only now decided to take my revenge, I did not kill him last night. How could I have? I was standing in the hallway. I couldn't have gotten over to you, then him, and back again without anyone have noticing. And I did not know any of the other tourists who were standing close to Chet."

Lana frowned, puzzled by Josepha's last comment. "What does that have anything to do with his murder?"

"It would have been impossible for any one person to have killed him. How could any one of us have turned off the lights, grabbed your hair comb, stabbed Chet, and then turned the lights back on in such a short amount of time? It was only dark for a few seconds, not minutes. There must have been two murderers up on that stage."

26

Lana Investigates

Josepha's words were a bombshell. One murderer would have been a lot to deal with, but two? Lana had to sit down and take it all in. Yet when the first students began to arrive, Josepha leaned in closer to Lana. "Please go now. Our first workshop begins in a few minutes. It might not be my passion, but it does pay the bills."

Lana nodded and crossed slowly to the exit, unable to stop thinking about what Josepha had said about there being two murderers present. Was it a coincidence that the lights went out when they did, or was it done intentionally, so as to give someone the chance to harm Chet unseen? The latter scenario did seem far more likely. If the murderer had simply taken advantage of the sudden darkness, then it was a lightning-fast reaction.

On her walk back to the hotel, her mind returned to the scene of the crime. According to the reconstruction they had done for the police inspector last night, Josepha, Amber, Serena, Becky, and Nick were definitely close enough to the light switches to have turned them off. And Ted, Erica, and Dwight were close enough to Chet to have harmed him. The participants in the other group, as well as the theater employees, were too far away to have done either.

As much as she wanted it to be an outsider this time, Lana had to face the fact that two of her guests had probably committed the crime.

"Great, so I'm probably leading a pair of murderers around this time, not just one, per usual," Lana grumbled aloud, causing a few passersby to give her a wide berth.

Either way, Lana figured the crime could not have been premeditated because the circumstances dictated that the murder had happened spontaneously. None of them knew the theater's windows had been blackened out, or that the needles attached to Lana's hair comb would be razor sharp.

Had the police inspector already arrived at the same conclusions?

She had hoped that the short walk back to their hotel would help clear her mind, but it didn't do the trick.

As much as she wanted to lock herself in her hotel room until the real killer was unmasked, she knew she had no choice but to keep the tour going. Yet, until she knew which of her guests were involved with Chet's death, she would not be at ease with any of them.

She was back at the hotel long before their taxi was scheduled to arrive to take them to the travel expo's last event. Instead of checking in with Randy, Lana used that time to see what she could find out about her guests. Before she could consider which two worked together to kill Chet, she had to figure out who wanted him dead the most.

Lana fired up her laptop, determined to find out more about her guests' motives. *Let's start with Dwight*, she thought. He was such an angry young man, and he had argued with Chet outside of his hotel room and during the discussion panel. Additionally, the conference center's security had detained him longer than necessary because he refused to leave Chet alone. Yet, Dwight steadfastly claimed that the travel writer was no good to him dead. Was it true, or was he trying to mislead the group and police into believing that he wouldn't harm Chet?

Unfortunately, Lana could not find anything online that connected the two men. It did not appear that they had ever worked together, nor had Dwight ever written about Only Footprints in his eMagazine. But the threats Dwight made about revealing the truth if Chet didn't do what he had promised made clear that the two men had met before the conference began. So what secret was Dwight threatening to expose if Chet didn't keep his end of their bargain?

She also couldn't find any proof that he, not Chet, had made the updates to the guidebook to Bulgaria, as Dwight claimed during the Q&A session. Did that mean that Dwight was a delusional liar? Or had he really visited all of the locations and Chet was lying about it in order to uphold his claim that he was Only Footprints' sole writer?

To top it off, Lana was still convinced that either Dwight or Ted had broken into Chet's room. Both men had been gone from the dinner party for an awfully long time. But why would either one do it—to scare Chet or to search for something? And did that mean that whoever broke into his room also killed him? Or were the two events unrelated? Whichever one of them did it, he must have a lot of pent-up anger—Chet's room had been savagely torn apart. Her money would go on Dwight, simply for that reason.

Lana made a note to ask Dwight about the Bulgaria guidebook and try to find out more about the break-in. Perhaps he would be forthcoming now that Chet was dead.

When she noticed that she only had a half hour left before the taxi arrived, she sped on to the next guest.

Amber was a bust. Though Chet had made degrading comments about her standpoints, the young blogger had not really seemed to care. What had she called him—a dinosaur or Neanderthal? It didn't really matter—the gist was the same. And she had done a marvelous job of putting him in his place during the discussion panel. No, Lana could see no reason to include Amber on her list of suspects.

Next up was Serena. She and Chet were embroiled in a vicious legal battle. As much as Serena claimed her logo looked nothing like Chet's, only a fool would agree with her. They were virtually identical.

An article in the *Financial Times* confirmed Lana's suspicions that this was not an open-and-shut case. According to the newspaper, millions of dollars were on the line, and the court's ruling could have implications for other trademark and copyright infringement cases.

Lana felt a shiver run up her spine. Could that lovely lady be a murderer? The lifestyle blogger acted as if the lawsuit was not a big deal, but it truly was. If the courts ruled in Only Footprints' favor, it would cost Serena millions. That would give her a serious motive. Was Serena lying when she said her lawyers were certain they were going to win this legal fight? Or was victory only guaranteed if Chet was out of the picture?

Lana pressed on, searching next for information about Ted Castle, Chet's former business partner. His departure from Only Footprints was fodder for many newspaper articles printed over the course of several months. In the beginning, Ted's departure was presented as if it was a mutual decision. After the fact, Ted claimed that Chet took advantage of his mental state and shorted his severance package. That correlated with what Erica, Ted's fiancée, had said about their split. Lana could find no follow-up articles that could clarify whether Ted had received more money. Again, that jived with what Erica said about it being an ongoing battle.

She tapped her chin, wondering what Ted would gain after Chet's death. For starters, it might be easier for him to prove that Chet had jilted him out of his fair share of Only Footprints' stock, without having Chet blocking his every move. And there was no one to bad-mouth his new website or try to hold up its release.

Lana jotted down a note to try to find out more about his split from Only Footprints and the noncompete clause he signed when leaving the company.

How did his fiancée fit into this picture? Lana typed in her full name but only found a LinkedIn profile that had not been updated in ages. According to the website, Erica was still working as a nurse at a private nursing home in Bellevue, Washington. There was no mention of Ted on her social media, nor could Lana find any articles linking the two together. So how did they meet—through her work as a nurse? It would be a bit creepy if they had begun an affair while his wife lay dying in their home, but it wouldn't have been the first time in human history that something like that had happened. If Chet had been poisoned, Lana would have moved Erica higher up her suspects list. But given the circumstances and the fact that Erica didn't seem to know anyone else in the travel industry or be particularly interested in it, Lana left her off of it.

Lana glanced over her to-do list. So far, Serena and Ted had the strongest motives.

Serena would have taken a hard hit financially, but from what Erica had said, Ted would have lost everything if Chet managed to block his website. Considering Chet was the driving force behind the lawsuit against Serena and had threatened to take legal action against Ted, both would most likely profit from his death.

But she had another pair to investigate, albeit reluctantly. What about Becky and Nick? They had told her that their television show was going to happen, whether Chet liked it or not. But they did react strongly when he made those cryptic threats during the panel discussion about their deal not being watertight. And they did pester Chet during the dance workshop. Then again, so did everyone else in her group.

What would be their motive for killing the guidebook writer? Even if Chet somehow did hinder their deal, what did it matter? They still had a popular blog and video subscription channel, both of which were heavily sponsored.

Lana ticked their names into the search engine, but before the results loaded, her phone's alarm went off, reminding her that the taxi was about to arrive. When she saw how many links their names brought up, she frowned at the screen. It was going to take quite a bit of time to sift through all the articles mentioning the dynamic duo.

She scanned the results for a mention of their upcoming television show, but didn't see any. Then again, Becky and Nick did say it had not been officially announced yet. Lana could imagine the television producer would want to keep it a secret until then.

To be continued, she thought as she sprung up and grabbed her purse before racing downstairs to meet up with her clients.

27

Wish Granted

The luncheon was a great distraction from her mental gymnastics. Not only was the food top-notch, several successful writers spoke during the meal, inspiring them to keep traveling and sharing their journeys with their readers and viewers.

By the time the speeches ended, Lana had almost forgotten about Chet. Unfortunately for her, the recently deceased travel writer was honored with an impromptu memorial service after dessert was served. Photos of Chet were projected behind the master of ceremonies, who quickly recounted the dead man's accomplishments.

When a photo of Chet taken outside of the Seville conference center flashed onto the screen, Dwight piped up, "Didn't Chet say at the opening dinner that he expected he'd keel over while traveling? Well, his last wish was granted—he died on the road."

His quip got a snigger out of the group.

"Too soon?" he asked when Lana gasped instead of laughing aloud.

The last image was of Chet's obituary in the *New York Times*. The short text recounted pretty much the same information the MC had just listed. However, it also mentioned that Chet had been set to host a new travel show, and that his unexpected death had thrown the production into limbo.

Becky and Nick gasped simultaneously and leaned their heads together, whispering frantically whilst gesturing towards the screen.

The text and the Sohos' strong reaction made Lana's brow crinkle, until she realized that an obituary was not a news item. Even though their contract had been signed, their roles as the new presenters had not been officially announced. The newspaper couldn't have known that the show was already moving forward without him.

After the lights went back up, Chet was quickly forgotten. While the waiters cleared their tables, the travel experts mingled and networked for one last time before the conference officially ended.

When her attempts at hobnobbing failed because no one had heard of her blog, Lana settled for watching her group work the room.

Becky and Nick were surrounded by a swarm of tour operators offering them free trips in exchange for coverage on the couple's influential video subscription channel. Serena was deep in conversation with a major retailer that wanted to sell her Barefoot Travel clothing line in their stores. Amber was smiling widely while listening to a fair-trade product wholesaler explain why he wanted to partner with her.

Ted seemed overwhelmed with the number of publishers suddenly interested in including their publications in his website's pay-to-read service. Rumor had it that Chet had been the driving force behind the new Only Footprints website, and now that he was dead, the entire project would be delayed indefinitely. Ted was clearly profiting from that turn of events, Lana realized, as she took in the circle of potential business partners surrounding him.

Standing close to Ted was Dwight, deep in conversation with a well-dressed man in his thirties. To Lana's amazement, Dwight had found a group of like-minded writers and publishers who were familiar with his work and enjoyed it. *There really was a readership for everything*, she thought. In contrast to the often-whiny tone he used when talking to her, Dwight was now in sales mode and quite convincing. From what she could overhear, Dwight was currently talking with a publisher interested in turning his eMagazine into a paper publication that would be distributed nationally.

At one point, the publisher Dwight was talking with turned to Ted and asked, "Are you really going to feature Dwight's work on your new website?

From your presentation, it didn't sound like you were going to feature critical voices. If that's true, I'll have to inform my network. I'm certain several would be interested in working with you."

Lana's ears perked up. That didn't make sense. Dwight's work was not at all appropriate for Ted's new venture, and the older man had made that quite clear on the first night of the conference.

Based on Ted's expression, he also seemed to disagree. His eyes were as wide as saucers and his cheeks were reddening fast. He shook his head slightly before recovering his composure. "Our focus hasn't changed. But we are looking forward to reading Dwight's weekly contributions. If you will excuse me, I see someone I need to talk to."

Ted began to sprint away, almost as if he was running away from the conversation. Erica grabbed his arm, stopping him in his tracks.

"What are you talking about? Dwight's work is not at all what you are looking for."

Ted glanced back at Dwight and said softly, "Can we discuss it later? I need to talk to a few more sponsors before this event finishes." He smiled widely and strode off towards a pair of trendily dressed twenty-somethings that Lana recognized as the leaders of a workshop on digital photography.

Why on earth would Ted suddenly look forward to working with Dwight? Lana watched Ted walk off, wondering what Dwight was getting up to. Had he thought up a new idea for a column—one more fitting for Ted's soon-to-be-live website? She wondered whether he was even capable of writing the sort of upbeat, somewhat frivolous articles that Ted wanted to feature.

Lana paled as her thoughts turned again to Chet's room being broken into. She was almost certain that one or both had been responsible, but Chet's death had pushed that now trivial crime aside. If Ted had broken in, and Dwight caught him doing it, he could be using that as a sort of blackmail, in order to get a weekly feature. That was what Dwight seemed to want most of all—to see his byline in the mainstream media.

It wouldn't be the first time Dwight had tried something similar, Lana realized. She had already heard him trying to blackmail Chet into doing his bidding. And now it seemed that he was holding something over Ted. Lana looked again to her guest, studying him critically. If Dwight had no qualms blackmailing someone to get what he wanted, would he also be prepared to murder for it?

28

Doing the Right Thing

When her guests regrouped at their table at the end of the networking luncheon, all seemed upbeat and positive about their future prospects.

Lana had to force herself to smile along. Considering she had spent most of her free time mulling over which one of them was capable of murder, it was rather hard to be relaxed and jovial in their presence. Yet after visiting their motives over and over in her mind, she still couldn't decide who stood to gain the most from Chet's death. The man had offended pretty much everyone he met. Was there anyone who did not want to see him out of the picture?

When the MC announced that they were closing the hall, Amber looked to Randy and Lana. "So this is the end of the conference, which means it's tour time. What do you have planned for us today?"

"This afternoon we get to explore Seville," Randy said. "Tomorrow we will be leaving early and traveling by bus to Cordoba. After that, we will visit Granada, Ronda, and Jerez before returning to Seville."

Amber's mouth was already open to protest when Randy added, "The tour bus runs on biofuel—I already checked."

The environmentalist nodded in approval and leaned back in her chair.

"Four cities in three days means it is going to be a whirlwind of a tour, but should give you a taste of Andalucía's finest sights. And this way we will be back in Seville for Good Friday. The last three days of our trip are all about

130

Semana Santa," Lana said, pumping her voice full of enthusiasm. Not that it was difficult to do so. She couldn't wait to witness at least part of the city's weeklong Easter celebrations and experience firsthand the centuries-old rituals steeped in symbolism and mythology.

Murmurs of approval and excitement circled the table.

"Our cab should be waiting by the main entrance for us. After we get back to the hotel, we will have an hour-long break. Then we are off to see more of this gorgeous city!" Randy said and rose, causing the rest to do the same.

During the short ride back to their hotel, Dwight's phone rang. He glanced at the screen and huffed, "Finally!"

"It took you long enough to call me back," he groused after answering the call. Seconds later, he raged into the phone, "No—you listen to me. The recording goes to *Good Morning America* tomorrow if you don't do what Chet promised."

Another short silence was followed up with, "I don't care how much it will cost! Chet should have done the right thing the first time. What will cost you more in the long term—reprinting the guides or having the truth coming out?"

As Dwight listened again, a thin smile spread across his lips. "That's what I thought. I look forward to seeing the digital proofs tomorrow."

When he hung up, he leaned back in his seat, a self-satisfied expression on his face.

"What was that all about?" Lana asked, recalling Dwight's fight with Chet, outside the travel writer's hotel room. He had been ranting about the truth coming out then, too. Whatever it was, Chet was adamant that it was only going to happen "over his dead body." And it did, indeed, sound as if Dwight was about to get his way. Despite having repeatedly claimed that Chet was no good to him dead, perhaps Dwight was lying, after all.

"You'll see soon enough," he said, then looked to Serena and Ted. "Suffice to say, no one messes with Dwight Anderson and gets away with it."

29

News Travels Fast

"Hey, Lana, do you have a minute?" Randy asked, after they had gotten their group back to the hotel and their hour-long break had begun.

"Of course." She waved him inside her room.

"How hands-on should we be with the group, do you think? They have all had far more experience traveling than I have, and I don't want to offend them. What if they get upset when we try to herd them onto the bus or to the next planned stop?" His tense tone reminded her of their first tour together in Paris. She hadn't seen Randy nervous around a group since. Yet, she too, wondered how they should approach leading these savvy travelers.

"I guess we will have to wait and see how needy they are. My biggest concern is the itinerary. Because of the conference, we don't have much time to explore Andalucía, so Dotty didn't ask if they had any special requests. But she did put together an action-packed schedule that will hopefully keep them too occupied to complain," Lana joked.

Randy laughed along. "I sure hope you are right. With the Easter processions at the end of the week, it is going to be busy everywhere, and we won't be able to be as flexible as we usually are. But this should be a fun week, I think. As long as we can keep the group spirit upbeat."

"That shouldn't be a problem, at least, as long as we aren't called into the police station. No one seems bothered by Chet's death. Hopefully we can all focus on enjoying Spain and the Easter celebrations, instead of the murder

132

investigation," she said.

Not that I'll have a chance to relax and enjoy the scenery, Lana thought, knowing she would have to stay alert for any slips of the tongue.

Before Randy could respond, Lana's phone rang. She stared at the number, momentarily surprised to see who was calling, before finally answering. "Jeremy? Is everything okay?" It was very early in the morning on the West Coast of America, where her friend lived.

"With me it is. I'm sorry to bother you, but my news editor just alerted me to breaking news. Do you have a moment?"

The news desk never sleeps, she thought. "For you I do. What's going on?"

"We have gotten word that that Chet Rogers was killed during an event organized by World Travelers Expo, but the details are still quite sketchy. Seeing as you are at the conference, I thought you might know something about it."

Lana plopped down on her bed and sighed. "Unfortunately, I do. He was murdered during a flamenco workshop my group and I were at."

"Are you certain it was murder?"

Lana's eyes fluttered shut as images of Chet's lifeless corpse filled her mind. "Yes, I am quite certain. He was stabbed in the neck with a *peinetas*—it's a hair comb attached to three sharp, needle-like pins." She couldn't bear to say that it was her comb that killed him. She was, after all, talking to a reporter, not just a friend.

Too late, she realized that she had already said too much. Chet could no longer write a degrading piece about her employer, but a newspaper article linking Wanderlust Tours to his murder investigation would not be good for business, either.

"Could you please not mention that we were there?" Lana begged. "I don't want Wanderlust's name sullied. The police consider everyone who was inside the theater a suspect, but that doesn't mean that anyone in my group did it."

Lana could almost hear Jeremy's brain running through his options. "Okay, I will leave your group's presence out because it isn't relevant to the article—at least, not yet. If anyone else publishes a list of those present, then I won't be able to hold my news staff back from doing the same."

"Thanks, my friend. I owe you one."

As soon as she hung up, a new thought made her groan. Speaking with Jeremy reminded her that she had not yet caught her boss up on this breaking news.

"Oh, no, we were up so late last night answering the police's questions, I forgot to call Dotty and tell her about Chet's death," she moaned.

Randy gritted his teeth. "Do you want me to do it?"

Lana laid a hand on his arm. "That's really sweet of you, but no. It's better that I do it. She's come to expect this sort of thing from me."

30

Cristobal Colón

"I didn't know his name was Cristobal Colón," Lana said as she took in the unusual tomb before them.

"Me, either," Randy whispered back.

After learning at school about his voyages during which he "discovered" the Americas, she had never expected that she would ever see his final resting place. Yet, here she was, in the Seville Cathedral, standing in front of the grave of Cristobal Colón—or, as she knew him, Christopher Columbus.

The *Mausoleo de Cristobal Colón* was one of the most interesting tombs she had ever seen. Four larger-than-life human figures held the explorer's coffin shoulder high. The pallbearers, each said to represent one of the four kingdoms of Spain during Columbus's life, bore crowns and were dressed in tunics and robes that reminded Lana of the Knights Templar. The statues' skin, eyes, and clothing had been painted quite realistically, making it seem as if the figures were frozen in place, instead of carved out of wood.

According to an information pamphlet, the tomb had originally been installed in Havana, but was moved to Seville after Spain lost control of Cuba. It fit well in with the rest of the decorations in this beautiful church, Lana thought. And there was plenty of room for the tomb. The Seville Cathedral was, after all, the largest Gothic cathedral in the world and a UNESCO-designated World Heritage site. The location was also fitting for Columbus's final resting place. Across the street was the Real Alcazar, the

Spanish royal palace where he had signed his contract with Queen Isabella to find a new route from Europe to Asia.

The tomb was placed across from the main altar, almost as if to allow the clergyman to gaze upon it during Mass. Behind it rose the thick stone walls of the cathedral, covered in frescoes and punctuated by several stained-glass windows. Lana shifted her gaze away from the tomb and across the groups of visitors pressing in all around them. The density of the crowds wandering around made it difficult to see all of the Wanderlust guests, but she trusted they were all inside somewhere, enjoying the views in their own way.

So far, no one in this group had expressed an interest in the guided tours, preferring to explore the sites on their own. It made Lana and Randy's jobs even easier and gave them a rare opportunity to take in the sites as tourists instead of guides.

"I want to check out the Chapter House," Randy said softly. "I'll meet you in the courtyard in an hour."

"Great, see you then," Lana replied before gazing around the massive church. She was glad they had a few hours to explore Seville before they traveled to Cordoba. When they returned, Holy Week would have begun and many of the city's monuments would be closed to the general public.

She slipped into a pew and stared up at the heavenly ceiling decorated with lattice-carved stone and ribs of brick. Rays of sun spilling in from the glass windows cast colorful light onto the ceiling and walls, drawing her eye to a massive clock placed high above Columbus's tomb. The timepiece was decorated with an angel made of gold. The heavenly being held a dove in one hand and a scythe in the other—symbols of life and death. The angel's attributes reminded Lana of her own predicament. Was she an angel of death? Murders didn't happen on every tour she led, but did occur often.

Her stomach clenched as she wondered how Dotty would react to Chet's death. Because Lana didn't want to wake up her boss with this dreadful news, she had sent her a message instead, asking Dotty to call at her convenience. Rushing things wouldn't bring Chet back or free their tour group from suspicion.

Catching sight of Becky and Nick, chatting animatedly while pointing at several carved figures, reminded her not to wallow in self-pity, but to enjoy her time in the city. She averted her gaze from the clock and joined the many tourists milling about the roomy interior.

She was drawn to the tall masterpiece of wood and gold adorning the cathedral's main chapel—the *Capilla Mayor*. The altarpiece, at least four stories tall, illustrated scenes from the life of Jesus and the Virgin Mary. In the center of the intricately carved display sat mother and child, each holding a flower or globe, respectively, in their hands. Their faces, arms, and hair were painted quite realistically, down to the blush in their cheeks.

Lana didn't know where to look, it was all so beautiful. She walked slowly in front of the magnificent artwork, trying to work out the stories represented. Soon she found herself a few feet away from Becky and Nick, also taking in the main altar.

Becky was holding two fingers from each hand up in front of her face so they formed the outline of a square. Curious as to what she was doing, Lana moved closer. Before she reached Becky, Nick slid up next to his wife.

"This would be a great shot," Becky enthused.

"Why would we want to film a video here? Our focus has always been on the hidden gems. Seville Cathedral is one of the most popular tourist attractions in the city," Nick said with disdain as he looked around the gorgeous space.

"True, but we can always use this footage for the B-roll. I want to get in touch with a local cameraman tonight, before we leave for Cordoba, but we have to create a shot list first," Becky pressed.

He groaned. "Why are you rushing things? The TV show has their own camera crew."

"What if this deal does not go through? We need to keep everything going as is, until we know it's a wrap," Becky hissed.

"With Chet out of the picture, nothing can hinder this deal, right?"

Lana's eyebrows shot up as she inched closer, hoping the couple was too involved in their conversation to notice her.

"Until we are on the air, I don't want to chance anything. We might need to keep shopping our show around. Have you called our agent yet today?"

"A half hour ago. He didn't pick up, so I left another message."

"Why won't he return our calls? I hope the producers aren't going to pull the same trick they did with Chet," Becky said before walking away from her husband, again using her fingers to visualize a camera's viewfinder.

Lana's curiosity shot into high gear. They had convinced her that Chet could not hinder their deal, but what if they were lying to her? If he had been a real threat to them, that would give them a strong motive to murder the man.

Wait a second, Lana thought. Even if Chet could have thrown a wrench in their plan, why would it matter now? Dead men could not present television shows. So why were the Sohos still concerned? Until she knew more about their television deal and Chet's involvement, Lana felt obligated to add her vlogging heroes to her suspects list.

31

Selfie Advice

"Oh, there you are, Lana!" Amber said loudly, causing several visitors in the church to turn towards her voice.

"What can I do for you?" she asked distractedly, her mind still on Becky and Nick's conversation.

"This smoke is horrid," Amber said, coughing into her hand as she did, for effect. A plethora of candles, lit by those seeking solace or help for a loved one, burned softly in the many racks set throughout the cathedral. Lana figured more candles had been lit than normal because of the massive influx of tourists in town for Semana Santa. But the tendrils of smoke didn't bother her. In fact, she rather liked the earthy sweet smell and thought it added to the atmospheric interior.

"You can't smoke cigarettes inside, so why is this allowed? I'm going outside."

"Oh, okay. We won't be much longer…" Amber strode towards the outer doors before Lana could finish responding. There were several churches on their itinerary, she realized, and from what she had read, large bowls of incense were burned during the Holy Week processions, as well. *Let's hope Amber doesn't turn her nose up at all of the churches and festivities.*

Luckily the rest of her guests had no problem with the scented air. Lana caught glimpses of them wandering around as she explored the many chapels and took in the impressive artwork. It would take hours to see everything this incredible church had to offer, and unfortunately they only had a few minutes left before they needed to get to their second site of the day.

When her phone began beeping, signaling that it was time to depart, Lana reluctantly followed the exit signs towards the Orange Tree Courtyard. The citrusy scent of their opening blossoms filled the air.

All of her guests were milling about, even Amber.

Lana crossed over to the young environmentalist. "Hey, Amber. I'm glad to see you didn't leave."

"This courtyard is so beautiful. And the orange blossoms smell so much nicer than the candle smoke. Did you know this space was part of a mosque that once stood on this site?"

"That's true. And the Giralda Tower was the minaret, at least the lower portions of it," Lana confirmed.

"Do we have time to climb the tower?" Amber asked.

Lana took in the long line of tourists already waiting for the chance to do the same. Because they had so little time to visit the site, Randy and Lana had chosen to skip climbing the tower first—as visitors were encouraged to do—and led their group straight inside the cathedral.

"I'm afraid we won't have time now because our tour of the royal apartments starts in a half hour. But we can buy you a timeslot ticket for later this week." Despite their guests' wishes to not take part in guided tours, that was the only way to access the private spaces within the Real Alcazar complex.

Amber looked longingly up at the tower, until Serena bounced up to her.

"I cannot wait to visit Real Alcazar—the interiors and gardens look gorgeous! We are going to get some great shots for our social media, Amber," she exclaimed.

The two young bloggers skipped forward towards the cathedral's exit, the tower climb forgotten.

Lana and the rest followed along. When they caught sight of Real Alcazar, Lana had to stop and stare. The building complex they were about to enter could not have been more different, architecturally speaking, than the church they had just visited. Whereas the cathedral's exterior was rather curvy and its roof a mass of pointy spires, Real Alcazar seemed be composed of thick stone and straight lines. Its crenellated walls reminded Lana of a medieval castle, not a royal palace.

They entered through a massive wall painted in red that led to the Puerta de León, the remains of a brick port named for a tile displaying a crowned lion carrying a cross and flag in his paws. The long wall's three doorless openings seemed to frame the courtyard beyond perfectly. After they entered the central square, Lana slowed her pace to better take in the building's exterior walls, partially covered in Moorish arches and tile mosaics.

Almost hidden behind tiled walls and lush green plants were several doorways and staircases leading to different spaces within the royal residence. Lana glanced around slowly, looking for anything indicating the location of their first destination.

Because Real Alcazar was the oldest European royal residence still in use today, she hadn't expected to see so many tourists milling around, most taking photos of the intricate architectural decorations, or studying their maps of the rather large complex. Through the crowds, she finally spotted a sign pointing towards the upper floors and the starting point of their guided tour of the royal apartments.

Her group headed up the staircase, snapping many photos of the colorful mosaic tiles covering the stairs and walls. After a brief wait, they were ushered into the palace's most private spaces. Each participant received a handheld audio guide programmed in their own language. A guard accompanied the group as they slowly walked through the royal residence.

The audio guide explained how Real Alcazar was originally built by the Moors as a military fortress in the eleventh century. The building complex fell into King Fernando III's hands after his forces recaptured Seville from the Moorish rulers in 1248. Christian rulers continuously renovated and added onto the site, which clarified why the various and palaces built over the centuries included Islamic, Gothic, Renaissance, Baroque, Mudejar, and Romantic elements.

The rooms were definitely fit for a king, Lana thought, recognizing that many of the Spanish monarchs had taken up residence here. The majority of the rooms' current decorations and furnishings were more Renaissance than Mudejar. Most walls were covered with richly woven tapestries created by a Dutch master, or family portraits and landscapes painted by Europe's finest artists.

It was only in the king's audience room that the original Moorish decorations dominated the space. The small room was an explosion of textures and patterns. Stylized seashells and vines covered parts of the walls, ceiling, and keyhole arches. The Moorish elements made the king's desk, positioned in the center of the space, seem even more majestic, Lana thought.

Their guide quickly ushered them through the many chambers comprising the royal apartment before leading them back to the entrance and wishing them a good day.

After their brief yet invigorating tour, the group split up, promising to meet back at the entrance in an hour. Lana knew it wasn't enough time to see everything, so she picked a direction and went for it. She followed the crowd left, slowly taking in the gorgeous spaces they wandered through, until she found herself in a hidden courtyard. The rectangular space was ringed by scalloped arches. Tiny trees and a narrow pond filled the tranquil space. Wooden panels on the ceilings were covered in geometric designs that represented the starry sky. The pools of water created a gorgeous play of light on the walls.

According to her map, it was the Maidens Courtyard. Lana took out her phone to snap a few pictures when she noticed Serena in one corner taking photos of herself against a multitude of backgrounds. Lana imagined that they would all be beautiful—the young woman was gorgeous.

As discreetly as she could, Lana took a few snaps of herself, hoping for one good selfie.

"Isn't this place phenomenal?" Serena gushed, surprising Lana from behind.

Lana dropped her arm, miserably aware that Serena had seen what she was doing. The young blogger was so pretty and self-assured, Lana felt inferior around her. The fact that she was nice and had a great mind for business made Lana even more acutely aware of her own shortcomings in life.

"You should hold your phone higher and extend your neck while you look up at the camera. The light falls better across your face that way." Serena took Lana's arm and extended it before raising the phone to the same height as her forehead and pointing it down. "Try that."

She did as she was told, grimacing as she snapped several selfies. When she reviewed the photos, she was surprised to see that she looked way better in these than she normally did, despite the unnatural angle required to take them.

When she looked away from her phone, Serena handed Lana hers. "Could you take a few wide shots for me? I want to get a picture of me standing in the middle of this gorgeous space. My followers really need to see it all."

Lana did as asked, taking numerous shots of Serena as she assumed various poses, most of which Lana was too shy and self-conscious to re-create in public.

After a few minutes, Serena bounced back to her and grabbed the phone out of her hand before greedily reviewing the shots. Lana looked over her shoulder as she did. Serena was even more gorgeous on film. It wouldn't have mattered if Lana had dropped the camera; the images of the young blogger would have turned out wonderfully, anyway.

"Excellent, I can use a few of those on my social media feeds. Thanks, Lana." The young blogger began to turn away, when she suddenly whipped around and asked, "Say, you write the *Travel Time* blog, right?"

"Yep."

"And you write about places you visit during your tours?"

Lana nodded.

"That's excellent. How much is your commission from Wanderlust?"

"Excuse me?"

Do you get a lot of cross-bookings through your website?" Serena patiently explained.

"I honestly don't know," Lana confessed.

"You really should keep an eye on your click-through rate. The information helps me determine my advertising fees. And I use affiliate links in my articles so I receive a percentage of the booking fee."

Lana blushed crimson when she realized what Serena meant. "I do include a link to the Wanderlust tour at the end of the blog post, but I haven't been keeping track of how many clicks it gets." Lana was still more concerned with attracting readers to her blog than promoting her boss's business.

"Oh, but you should. I am partnering with a travel agency that wants to promote their trips on my social media. I think it's going to be a large source of advertising revenue, seeing as many of my followers are travelers. And what better way to inspire them to book a trip than showing them amazing photos of the destinations the company flies to and their gorgeous hotels?"

"Are you going to lead the tours, as well?"

"Heavens, no! I have better things to do than lead a bunch of strangers around," she laughed, then stopped short, seeming to remember why Lana was there. "They are paying for advertising space, not my time. I'll post the photos they send me and include information about the places they visit, but I won't be one of the guides or guests."

"How much do you charge?"

Serena chuckled softly. "I am not allowed to disclose that amount, but I assure you they are paying a hefty price. Considering I have over thirty-two million followers on Instagram, Twitter, TikTok, and Facebook combined, I think I'm worth every penny."

Lana's jaw about dropped to the floor, as she tried to fathom so many followers, but Serena didn't seem to notice.

"My first clothing line, Barefoot Travel, launched last year, and it has already made me a millionaire. Partnering with a travel agency is just another way of leveraging the marketing potential of my audience. My By Serena brand of travel-friendly makeup cases and cosmetics that I am launching later this year is sure to be even more successful."

Lana was in awe. This young woman was far more business savvy than she would ever be, and Serena was half her age. And yet, she was embroiled in a nasty legal battle with Chet that, according to the newspapers, could cost her millions. What would his death mean for her lawsuit? Lana figured this was as good a time as any to find out.

"Did it bother you that Chet accused you of copying his Only Footprints logo in order to profit off of his popularity?" Lana dared to ask.

Serena threw her nose up. "Not really. It's never nice to be accused of something you did not do, and especially in the media. Luckily, my followers don't pay attention to Neanderthals like him." A twisted smile briefly settled on her lips. "I guess I should have used the past tense."

Lana looked to the ground, uncomfortable, as she asked her next question. "The first night we were in Seville, I saw you go into Chet's hotel room. Were you two having an affair?"

Serena's face puckered up as if she had just bitten into a lemon. "No! That is disgusting. Look, I know they say no publicity is bad, but I don't want to get mixed up in a lawsuit. It's not good for my karma or my number of followers. My lawyers advised me that it might be better for my career if I paid Chet off so as to avoid further negative publicity—as long as he agreed to drop the lawsuit and sign a confidentiality agreement. I went to his room to try to bribe him into signing the forms. But he wasn't going for it because he wanted to embarrass me publicly. He really was a horrible man."

"Will the lawsuit continue, now that he's dead? Or will it be dropped?"

A shadow crossed Serena's face. "I honestly do not know. Even before Chet died, my lawyers were certain that we would have won the case if it had actually gone to trial. They have already talked to Chet's lawyers about cutting a deal. Now that Chet's gone, I am hoping this whole nasty business will be wrapped up sooner than later."

"Is that why you killed him?"

"No! If we had lost, it would have been a financial hit, but not a devastating one."

Lana cocked one eyebrow at her. "I'm sorry, but I don't agree with your lawyers. Your logos are almost identical, and there are millions on the line. Are you seriously telling me that you just walked away from his room and let it go?"

Serena glared at Lana, steely-eyed. "Yes, that is what I am saying. The profits from my By Serena brand should offset any losses I might suffer. That's why I pushed its launch six months forward. So far things are looking quite promising. I've already had more retailers interested in stocking my travel cases and cosmetics than I have for my clothing line. I had no reason to harm Chet."

Despite Serena's adamant protest, Lana wasn't buying it completely. Serena may have convinced herself that Chet couldn't touch her, but there was too much money involved to be so nonchalant about the chances of losing. Lana knew firsthand that people murdered for less. As much as she wanted to shorten her list of suspects, Lana could not scratch Serena off of it quite yet.

<h1 style="text-align:center">32</h1>

Disappointing Dotty

Before Lana could question Serena further, her phone began to ring. *Darn it,* she thought as she fumbled around in her purse for it. Before she could find it, Serena scurried away. *My questions must have hit a nerve. I need to follow up on that later.*

"Hello," she whispered and crossed over to a window, hoping palace security would let her be. The guards were not kind to tourists talking loudly on their cellphones, and she'd already seen them escort one particularly boisterous visitor out of the palace.

"Hey, Lana. Just returning your call. Please don't tell me you need a lawyer," Dotty said.

"No! At least, not yet."

Dotty's disappointed sigh traveled through the international line. "What happened?"

"It wasn't one of our group that got killed this time. Chet Rogers was murdered during our flamenco workshop."

"What!" Lana could hear her boss dropping onto her couch. "I cannot believe this," Dotty muttered.

"The police have taken our passports so we can't leave Spain until they have had a chance to investigate more thoroughly."

Dotty gasped. "Wait—you are all suspects? This is worse than normal."

"I guess technically we are. But the police took the passports from every

147

tourist who was present in the theater at the time of Chet's death. I can't imagine they can keep them for long. Especially if they don't find any evidence tying any of us to the murder. I expect that once we get back to Seville, he will return them to us," Lana reasoned.

"I suppose you're right. It's good you called to let me know what is going on. If there's anything else I can do for you, like arrange for a lawyer, do let me know. I'll keep my phone on at night, just in case you need help in a hurry."

"Let's both keep our fingers crossed that no one in our group will require legal assistance before the end of the tour," Lana agreed before clearing her throat. There was one more thing she needed to sort out with Dotty before letting her boss get on with her day.

"This might not be the right time to bring this up, but Chet and I argued in public the day before he died. He claimed that the travel expo organizers told him that you had pulled a bunch of strings to get me on the panel. He was so incensed that a nobody like me was there, that he was going to write a nasty article about Wanderlust Tours. Unfortunately, quite a few people from the conference heard us argue, which gives me a motive."

Along with my hair comb being the murder weapon and me landing on Chet's corpse right before the lights went back on, she thought, unable to tell Dotty the entire truth. She could recount all the sordid details once she was back in Seattle—assuming the police cleared her of this crime.

"Before the police question me again, I need to know if there is any truth to his claims. Did you use your pull as a sponsor to get me on the panel?"

Instead of a quick and strong denial, Lana was surprised by the lengthy silence that followed her question.

"I wouldn't have worded it that way," Dotty finally said.

Lana's breath caught in her throat. "Wait, so Chet wasn't lying?" Dotty was such a stickler for rules and regulations, she couldn't believe that her boss would even consider doing such a thing.

"Yes and no. One of the conference organizers called me after that blogger broke her leg because she was part of your original tour group. She was moaning about having to find a new blogger for their 'emerging voices' slot at the last minute, so I suggested you."

"But why? I don't blog full time, like all the other panelists do."

"The organizer did want to check out your work before offering you the slot. When she called back, she did say that she wasn't certain you were the right person because you didn't have a large body of work behind you. I suppose me being one of the main sponsors does hold some sway, so I asked her to overlook that detail and book you in anyway. I guess some people might see that as using my influence to get what I want. I choose to view it as helping a valuable employee and friend advance her career."

"Oh, no. Chet was right," Lana moaned. "It was so obvious to everyone present that I was not qualified enough to be sitting on that panel! The rest had all sorts of great tips and advice to share. Heck, they all earn a living with their social media and websites, and I'm just a beginner! It was borderline embarrassing."

"Look, I didn't beg them to give you the slot. They called me, remember?" Dotty huffed. "All I did was mention that you were already going to be at the conference because of the tour, and that your *Travel Time* blog qualified you to be an 'emerging voice.' I know how much extra attention the panelists get and hoped this would help propel your blog to a higher level. There is no harm in helping a friend, is there? Would you have preferred that I had snubbed you and recommended another blogger to the organizer?"

"When you put it like that…" Lana's voice trailed off. How could she ever be mad at Dotty? The woman had a heart of gold, sometimes to a fault. She couldn't have known that Lana's inexperience would cause her to feel out of place, or that it would have made her a target for Chet.

"Sorry, you're right. I'm hugging you through the phone right now. I'll keep you updated on the murder investigation."

"Lana? Before you go, I have a small favor to ask," Dotty said in a soft voice. "Could you pick up a gift for Willow's baby? Little Zoe's keeping her up so much, Willow is like a zombie these days and is feeling rather depressed. I know it's my fault that you aren't in Seattle right now, but she would really appreciate knowing you were thinking of her."

Lana's stomach sank. Dotty's request was a painful reminder of another situation Lana had managed to mess up. Why hadn't she thought of buying something special for Willow or her baby? Despite all the extra tours she was working, she could have made time to call her best friend. Yet since Zoe had been born, her new daughter was all that Willow wanted to talk about. Lana had never been good with infants and didn't know the first thing about raising them. She simply didn't know what to say when they did talk. She knew it should not matter, that Willow would be happy enough that she had bothered to call, but it did. As much as she knew she needed to be a better friend to her bestie, she didn't know how to.

"I did see an adorable flamenco dress for babies in the hotel's gift shop."

"That would be perfect!" Dotty squealed. "You can give it to her in person, after your next tour ends."

"True, after Spain and Germany, I do have a two-week break, don't I?" Lana said, immediately relaxing a little. As much as she loved her job, it was good to have a few weeks off now and again so she could recharge her batteries.

Randy rounded the corner and pointed at his watch when he caught sight of her.

"It looks like we need to get our group moving," Lana said. "I'll give you a call if we need your help."

<h1 style="text-align:center">33</h1>

<h1 style="text-align:center">Caregivers</h1>

When Lana's tour group exited Real Alcazar and walked over to Plaza de España, the sun broke through the last remaining clouds and shone brightly down on a row of horse-drawn carriages parked around a large tiered fountain. A wide canal circled the space, its waters filled with tourists in ancient-looking rowboats. Ornately painted tiles covered the many bridges, brightening up the square with bursts of orange, white, blue, and green.

The plaza was actually a semicircular space enclosed on one side by a massive orange-stone building constructed to house the Ibero-American Exposition in 1929. Now it was home to several government offices. Lana imagined those city workers had the best view in Seville.

When a horse-drawn carriage clip-clopped past their group, Lana tensed up, hoping that Amber would not launch into a tirade accusing the drivers of animal abuse. Luckily, she and Serena seemed far more interested in taking selfies in front of the canal that gave this square the nickname the "Venice of Seville."

To the right of the plaza was Parque de Maria Luisa, a vast public park whose paths twisted under the shade of glorious old trees, and tall flowering shrubs provided shelter from the hot sun.

"It is so beautiful," Erica enthused as she pointed to the boats. "Oh my, Ted, look at that. Maybe we could rent one of those later? It does look romantic."

To Lana, it did look like fun, but not necessarily romantic. Most of the rowers seemed to be struggling to get their craft moving in the right direction, and for a few, tensions were running high. Luckily most seemed to laugh off the bumps from other boats.

"You're right, kitten. I'm going to get a few shots of these, then we can go see how much it costs to rent one."

Erica dug their camera out of her bag, and then Ted wandered off, snapping several shots as he went. She smiled at Lana. "It is beautiful here. I'm glad the weather's been cooperating. I'll be brown before the week's end at this rate!"

"How true!" Lana grinned and turned her face towards the sun. "I didn't expect to have to wear suntan lotion in April. Say, are you two enjoying the trip so far?"

"That church and palace were both amazing." Erica glanced over at Ted, still out of earshot, before adding, "Honestly, I'm just glad we are done with the conference. I know it was important to Ted's career, but it was pretty boring."

"I didn't have the impression that you were in the travel industry. How did you two meet?" Lana asked, hoping Erica would not be offended by her impertinence.

Erica glanced uncomfortably at the ground before answering in a soft voice, "I was a nurse at a private hospital for several years before I began working with a temporary agency. Ted hired me to nurse his first wife, after she was moved back home. During the year I cared for her, we shared so much. I know it's not professional, but after a few months, I began to have feelings for him. And I suspected that he felt the same way about me. But we didn't act on those feelings until after she had passed!"

"Oh, I see," Lana replied, uncertain whether to feel revolted or enchanted by the fact that Ted fell in love with the woman who nursed his dying wife.

Luckily for her, Ted soon returned with a triumphant look on his face. "Those boats floating under the tiled bridges make the best shots. Why don't we walk around the rest of the canal so I can get a few more?"

"That's a great idea. Do we have any more tours lined up for today?" Erica asked.

"No. We have dinner reservations at eight, but the rest of the afternoon is free."

"Great! We'll see you back at the hotel before then," Erica replied and pulled her fiancé away.

Before she was out of view, Erica glanced back worriedly and bit her lip when she noticed Lana watching them.

What was she hiding? Lana wondered. Or was Erica simply embarrassed about how she and Ted had met? *As if I need more suspects*, Lana thought as a feeling of hopelessness settled over her.

34

Behind the Mask

April 12—Day Five of the Wanderlust Tour Cordoba, Spain

Lana stared at the enormous structure before them. The Mosque-Cathedral of Cordoba, or Mezquita, was far larger and more imposing than she had expected it to be. The building's exterior seemed to be a cross between a church and a palatial home, she thought as she helped herd her group into the Orange Tree Courtyard, which housed the entrance to the Mosque-Cathedral.

It had been an early start, and most of her guests had slept during the hour-long ride drive. Only Dwight had been awake enough to want to chat, specifically with Serena and Ted. Both ignored him, choosing shut-eye over conversation, to Dwight's clear displeasure.

Their bus had dropped them off in front minutes before the monument was scheduled to open. In Lana's mind, this was going to be the highlight of the tour. She was fascinated with the photos of the interior she had seen and the building's complex history as both mosque and Catholic church.

Lana had read that the structure had originally been built as a mosque in the eighth century. In 1236, after the Moors had been driven out of Seville, a tiny Catholic church had been built in the center of the enormous mosque. Lana couldn't wait to see this combination of two religions and their distinctive architectural traditions firsthand.

Hidden behind the massive walls surrounding the courtyard were pencil-thin cypress and palm trees towering above the orange trees. Their tiny petals scented the air and covered the path leading to the Mosque-Cathedral's entrance. The arches lining the patio perfectly framed the bell tower soaring above them. Its creamy orange stone contrasted beautifully with the bright blue sky.

She had been looking forward to seeing the structure's interior but hadn't thought about the garden. Apparently, she wasn't the only one enjoying the views.

"Oh, wow, would you look at those palm trees?" Becky squealed. "A slow pan across this courtyard would make a great opening shot."

"I thought we agreed to hold off on making a shot list until after we talk with our agent," Nick growled. His intensity caught Lana's attention. So far, he had been the most relaxed guest on this tour. Why did Becky's comments upset him so?

Becky turned on Nick, her eyes already narrowing, until something behind her husband made her expression instantly soften.

A group of twenty-somethings were rapidly approaching the Sohos, their cameras and phones already in hand.

"You're Becky and Nick Soho, right?" a giggling young woman asked.

When Becky nodded, she squealed and turned to her friends. "Told you! Could I get a picture with you two?" The young lady didn't wait for a response and was already moving so that she stood in between the couple. The Sohos moved apart and threw their arms over her shoulders, smiling brightly as several photos were taken of the threesome.

"Thanks so much!" the young lady exclaimed as another woman rushed to take her place.

Dwight walked over to the group, standing next to Lana as he watched the scene unfold. The sour expression on his face made her nervous. So far Dwight seemed to be picking fights with anyone who appeared to be more successful than himself. From what she could see, Serena, Ted, Amber, and the Sohos worked tirelessly to promote their brands and improve their crafts. *Why does he feel entitled to the same level of success that they have?* she wondered. It was too bad that Dwight's jealous streak made it impossible for him to be genuinely happy for others.

"You aren't going to pester Becky and Nick, are you?" she asked in a teasing tone, hoping to defuse whatever tension the young man was feeling.

"No. But I am amazed at how shallow their followers are. Don't they see the truth?"

What was it with Dwight? Ted and Serena had been doing a great job of giving him the slip, so now he had chosen a new target, Lana mused. "What have they done to upset you?"

"It's all about keeping up appearances with those kinds of people. They claim to be this super-successful duo, but in reality they are on the verge of bankruptcy. It's amusing to see how they keep up the façade."

"What do you mean? They have millions of subscribers and tons of sponsors. How could they be almost bankrupt?"

"That may be, but they'll need twice the amount they now have to pay off all of their debts."

Lana frowned. *What a petty little man.* "Why would you say such a thing?"

Dwight's riotous laugh caught her off guard. "They got to you, too, eh? They are charismatic. That's why I keep my distance and don't try to make friends with these influencers. I know you don't trust me and think I'm lying about your buddies Becky and Nick, but they aren't all they claim to be. Keep looking behind the mask, Lana. It's the only way to survive in this industry."

Scratch that, he's not petty. He's paranoid, she thought. "Whatever, Dwight."

She turned to walk away, when he added, "They have spent close to a half million on their videos, and most were uploaded before sponsors began flocking to them. Their corporate nest egg couldn't cover everything, so they took out loans, maxed out credit cards, and double-mortgaged their house to pay for it all. From my research, they are still up to their eyeballs in debt, even with their recent influx of sponsors."

Dwight's wicked smile turned Lana's stomach. "Why have you been investigating them?"

"I am writing an exposé about them. It is a happy coincidence that they are on this trip. Now I have a chance to get to know my prey better. They do a great job of faking it."

Lana's eyebrows knitted together. Was he telling the truth or was this another jealous outburst?

Apparently Dwight noticed her indecision. "You don't believe me, do you? I'll email you my rough draft." Dwight wagged his finger in her face. "No sharing—it's still confidential. This article is going to bring me into the spotlight, trust me. And it is just the start. My name will be featured in the mainstream media soon enough."

"How are you going to do that?"

"Never you mind."

"Do you mean Ted's new website? How did you manage that? I thought he wasn't a fan of your style."

Dwight's eyes narrowed, and he turned to walk away from her.

Lana tried another line of questioning. "I saw you fighting with Chet in his room, the second day we were in town. What were you arguing about? And what was with that temper tantrum you threw at the panel discussion?"

Dwight whipped around to face her. "I wasn't throwing a temper tantrum! I was telling the truth—I updated the last Only Footprints guidebook to Bulgaria, not Chet. And he refused to credit me in the guidebook, as he had promised."

"Why would he do that?" Lana asked.

"Because he had to keep up the appearance that he was the sole writer. Which is not at all true, by the way. I know several freelancers who have worked for him. One even warned me that Chet had reneged on their agreement, as well, and refused to credit him in the France update. I thought that guy was trying to scare me off so he could take the gig. I should have listened."

Lana's puzzled expression caused Dwight to pull out his phone.

"I recorded my conversation with Chet, in case he did leave my name out," Dwight said before playing a short recording of a phone conversation for her. Dwight was not lying—Chet had clearly promised him a byline in the Bulgaria guidebook if he completed the work on time.

"So why did he leave your name out?"

Dwight huffed. "Chet claimed that my work was not up to his standard and that he had to rewrite so much of it that it was his own. That's ridiculous, of course. And I need that byline! Chet refused to listen, but his estate did. They sent me the digital proofs of the soon-to-be-updated guide, with my name in it, as promised. Now I don't have to share this recording with *Good Morning America*."

Gotcha! Lana thought. After all his moaning about how Chet's death would destroy his life, it had actually made it easier for him to get what he wanted. "So you did benefit from Chet's death?"

"No, that's not what I meant! You are just as bad as the rest, twisting my words like that. I didn't know his estate would bend so easily." Dwight's tone grew increasingly higher as his hands balled into fists and he moved slowly closer towards her.

Lana took a step back, momentarily worried that Dwight might strike her. Before she could react, Randy called out to them.

"Hey, folks. We are all set to go. The rest are waiting for us by the entrance." Randy's tone was as casual as could be.

When she looked to Dwight, expecting to see him foaming at the mouth, he seemed at ease again. Had she imagined his anger? Lana wasn't taking any chances. She rushed over to her fellow guide and linked her arm around his.

"Great, thanks, Randy!" She looked back at her guest, who was watching Lana as they walked away. If anyone on their tour had killed Chet, her money was on Dwight Anderson.

35

Mother Earth

Lana made a point of avoiding Dwight as they entered the Mezquita. Once they entered the mosque, the sight before her cleared her mind completely. The plethora of red and white arches repeating all around her was incredibly surreal. A deep serenity and peacefulness Lana had never experienced overcame her.

Lana was glad that Dotty had insisted they leave Seville early so they would be one of the first groups to enter the Mosque-Cathedral. The longer they were inside, the busier it became. Despite the no-talking rule and repeated announcements asking visitors to be quiet, most tourists couldn't help whispering to each other. Lana understood completely; there was something magical about standing inside of this space.

As she moved through the massive space towards the church in the middle, the type of arch changed slightly, becoming more stylized the farther she walked. According to her guidebook, the original mosque had been expanded several times in the ninth and tenth centuries, and the then-rulers had left their marks on the decorations.

The Catholic church in the center was tiny but still a glorious sight, made even more extraordinary by its location. The frescoes gracing its walls were exquisite. Its inclusion made the structure even more of a unique and almost otherworldly place. She wished they had time to go back and visit again. *One day,* she thought, *and next time I'll bring Alex.*

159

When they walked back outside into the harsh afternoon sunlight, the spell was broken, and reality came crashing back. Her thoughts automatically turned to her present dilemma: who killed Chet Rogers?

Despite Dwight's protests to the contrary, Lana could not cross him off her suspects list. Ted and Serena were also strong candidates. Lana blew out her cheeks. Her suspects list seemed to be getting longer, not shorter.

When she caught sight of Amber, Lana figured she might as well interrogate the environmentalist. Though she did not think that Amber was the killer, it was still important to talk to her about Chet's death. Perhaps she had heard or seen something that would incriminate another member of her group.

They had lunch reservations at a restaurant Dotty claimed had the best tapas in Andalucía. Because it was so close to the Mezquita, they decided to walk to the restaurant. Their path would lead them over another of Cordoba's tourist attractions, the Roman Bridge.

They exited onto the streets of Cordoba and quickly made their way to the water's edge. Lana had to stop to better take in the ancient bridge straddling the Guadalquivir River. Its fat, almost triangular ramparts reminded Lana of a ship's hull.

As they walked, she made a point of scooting up close to Amber. After learning that the environmentalist had not seen or heard anything of interest during the flamenco workshop, Lana finally dared to ask, "What do you think about Chet being murdered?"

Amber shrugged her shoulders. "Who cares? I mean, I don't approve of murder, but the guy was a real jerk. Some would say that he had it coming."

"He did say some pretty mean things about you and your blog," Lana reasoned.

"Dinosaurs like that don't get why my generation needs to be so loud and in your face about the world's environmental crisis. We didn't cause this environmental catastrophe, but we are the ones who have to deal with its effects."

Lana had to force herself from rolling her eyes. Truth be told, she was also getting irritated by the young woman's constant critiquing. "I can imagine it must be frustrating to see so many destructive acts happening all around you. But do you have to point them all out?"

Amber looked up at her, disappointment in her eyes. "You don't get it, do you?"

Lana blushed, feeling quite old.

"If no one says anything, then no one will change. It's all about education. Most people want to save our planet, but they just don't know how. Restaurants and hotels won't choose our climate over profits unless their clients demand they do so. That's why blogs, like mine, are so important. I don't want to have to keep harping on these issues, but someone has to."

Lana suddenly understood why Amber had been pestering everyone to change their behavior. Her methods may be slightly annoying, but she was right. It was her generation that was stuck with the effects of earlier generations' overconsumption.

She looked to the young blogger with new respect. "Thanks for looking out for Mother Earth, Amber."

"You're welcome."

36

Off the Tour

Their evening ride to Granada through the Sierra Nevada Mountains was spectacular. The moonless night, high altitudes, and clear skies meant more stars were visible than Lana had seen in years. It felt as if they were driving through a field of sparking white lights, framed by the silhouette of the mountain range, its jagged peaks hovering high above the horizon. She was almost certain they could see the Milky Way, its thick cloud of stars and galaxies evident even from the road.

As they entered Granada, she recognized the Alhambra, lit up by bright spotlights, towering over the city and dominating their view. Lana couldn't wait to visit it tomorrow with their guests.

After they had gotten their group checked into their hotel, their guests wandered over to the lobby bar to order a nightcap. Everyone except Dwight sat at one table; the angry young writer took a seat at the bar. Lana hoped he didn't drink too much tonight. They had to leave the hotel fairly early in the morning.

Randy and Lana grabbed a drink and slipped into a corner booth to confer about the next day's scheduled events. Because they had an early timeslot to visit the Alhambra, they figured their group would want to spend the entire morning wandering around the massive complex. Afterwards, a delicious lunch and a walk through the narrow streets of the Albaycin neighborhood to see its many historic Moorish palaces were on the agenda.

They had just finished for the night and were heading towards the elevators, when Ted and Erica stood up and waved goodnight to the rest. When the couple passed them by, Lana heard Ted say, "Now that Chet's dead, nothing is standing in my way."

Lana's stride faltered. Seeing as Ted was high up on her suspects list, she moved in behind him, matching his pace in the hopes that he might slip up and say more, when Dwight crossed their path. The young man had again drank too much too fast and was weaving his way towards the elevators.

Ted's eyes narrowed as he watched Dwight stumble his way across the lobby. He kissed Erica, then said, "Excuse me, darling. It's time to cut away one last shackle."

He sprinted to catch up to Dwight, who was almost by the elevators. Ted grabbed his arm and said something to Dwight. The sneer on the older man's face shocked Lana. *What is going on now?* she wondered. So far, Ted had been the epitome of a gentleman and had kept his cool in every kind of situation.

Randy, too, sensed that something was afoot. He walked back to Lana, both watching their guests' conversation play out. Whatever the two men were saying to each other, it was clearly becoming more heated by the second.

"What is Dwight's problem?" Randy asked, watching the men warily. "He seems to have a beef with pretty much everyone on our tour."

"I don't know, but I don't like it. There is something not quite right with that one. His behavior is becoming borderline violent. If he keeps it up, we may be forced to kick him off the tour."

"If he gets physical with anyone, he's done, as far as I'm concerned," Randy said adamantly. "And I am certain Dotty would agree wholeheartedly."

Lana nodded emphatically. "You are absolutely right. There is no discussion needed, if he crosses that line. Let's just hope it doesn't go that far."

Erica was also rooted to the spot, her eyes on her fiancé as his and Dwight's voices rose higher, the longer the conversation went on.

When Dwight stepped close to Ted, Lana had a bad feeling that this situation was escalating. "Should we do something?" Lana asked. "Maybe ask them if they enjoyed their day, you know, something to distract them?"

"That's a good idea," Randy answered, his eyes fixated on their guests. "But let me do it. I don't want them to take out their anger on you."

He took a step towards their guests when Dwight suddenly screamed, "Chet's death doesn't change our agreement! You can't back out now, unless you want to be a suspect in his murder. You either, Serena!" Dwight yelled in the direction of the lobby bar.

When Serena used her hand to shield her face from his view, Dwight exploded, "You can't avoid me forever! You said we were going to help each other. It's been a one-way street so far."

He spun around to face Ted, a menacing expression etched on his face. "You two think you are better than me, don't you? Well, guess what—you are not!" Dwight pushed Ted hard against his chest, knocking the older man backwards.

Erica raced over to her fiancé as the two guides tore over to Dwight.

"What do you think you are doing?" Lana cried as she spread out her arms and legs so Dwight couldn't get past her.

"None of your business," Dwight growled.

When he rushed at her, she glared at him, standing her ground. "Are you going to hurt me, too? We don't tolerate physical violence. You are off the tour."

"You can't kick me out!"

"Yes, she can," Randy said as he stepped in between them.

"It's Serena and Ted that are in the wrong—not me! I was only trying to get them to do what they promised. I shouldn't have pushed Ted, but he shouldn't have lied to me."

Dwight looked to Ted and Erica, who were slinking away from the younger man.

"There is no excuse for what you did," Lana stated resolutely. "I am not changing my mind."

"The police have my passport, I can't leave the country even if I wanted to," Dwight retorted.

Drat! Lana clicked her tongue. He was right, none of them could leave Spain at the moment. "That may be so, but you are not welcome to join in the scheduled activities or come near anyone in our group. I wouldn't be surprised if Ted presses charges! What is wrong with you? Why are you fighting with everyone?"

"It doesn't concern you," Dwight stated as he turned to glare at Ted and Serena.

The pair were now standing by the elevator doors, pushing the up button repeatedly as they glanced back at Dwight. Erica stood behind Ted, staring blankly ahead as if she was in a daze. When the doors opened, Serena sprung inside, and Ted pulled Erica in after her.

"Does this have anything to do with Chet's murder?" Lana asked, grasping at straws. She truly did not understand why Dwight was so aggressively targeting Serena and Ted.

"I didn't kill him, if that is what you are implying!" Dwight's voice rose an octave. "My beef with Serena and Ted concerns other matters—none of which are your business. I simply refuse to be taken advantage of any longer. I lived up to my end of the bargain; now it is time for those two to do the same."

"I don't care what they did to you, there is no reason to resort to violence." She shook her head in disappointment, hoping Dwight would hang his head in shame. Instead, his facial muscles seemed to harden, and his fists were balling up again. It was quite clear that he was not remorseful for his actions. In fact, he was staring at her as if she was in the wrong.

"Let me be crystal clear. If you do not leave the group alone, I will call the police," Lana stated as firmly as she could, hoping that her mentioning bringing in the authorities was enough for him to get the message and let them be. However, based on his defiant expression, Lana feared he didn't get it.

He stalked off towards the staircase, shaking his fist as he went. "You haven't heard the last of Dwight Anderson!"

"Are you okay? You're shaking," Randy said as he squeezed her shoulder lightly.

"That was horrible. Who does Dwight think he is?" Lana shook her head, still in disbelief.

"He really does have an anger management issue. I know the security guards were certain he would have attacked Chet again during the panel discussion, given the chance. That's why they kept him in their custody for the duration of the discussion. When I picked him up, the guards told me that had to lock him in the broom closet because he kept trying to sneak out of their office."

Lana shivered, glad that their confrontation with Dwight had ended as well as it had. "Angry and tenacious—that is a dangerous combination."

"Did you understand any of that gibberish he was saying about Serena and Ted owing him?" Randy asked. "I can't imagine either one of them would want to be associated with Dwight—especially in light of his temper."

"I can't imagine that either. It's as if he's blackmailing them, but with what?" Lana mused. Despite both men's assertions to the contrary, she was fairly certain Ted had broken into Chet's room and Dwight had seen him do it. That would explain how he weaseled his way into Ted's new website. But what dirt did he have on Serena?

Lana mulled over the possibilities, but she came up blank.

If she couldn't get the truth out of Dwight, then she would have to try wheedling it out of Serena or Ted.

Randy must have sensed the struggle raging inside of Lana because he turned to face her, gazing at her quizzically. "What are you planning, Lana Hansen? And how can I help?"

Lana smiled, grateful to have a friend to confide in.

37

Tour Must Go On

April 13—Day Six of the Wanderlust Tour in Granada, Spain

After getting Randy up to speed on her suspicions as to who might have killed Chet and why, Lana felt more secure. Saying her thoughts aloud helped clarify things in her head. And it was nice to have someone watching her back.

Their late-night talk made Lana realize that she needed to know more about what Dwight was holding over her guests. Seeing as it was already midnight by the time she and Randy finished chatting, Lana decided to leave her guests be for now. *Tomorrow is a new day*, she told herself before drifting off to sleep.

The morning came too soon. The dark circles under her eyes were a reminder of her lack of progress. Lana feared she would only be able to sleep soundly again after she had unmasked Chet's killers.

Because they were leaving so early, breakfast had been a rushed affair that had left her no time to talk to Serena or Ted. Luckily, Randy was more than willing to help her to create an opportunity for her to do so during their tour of the Alhambra.

Their minibus climbed slowly up the steep hill upon which the Alhambra was built, giving them a preview of the day's destination. It seemed to go on forever. Lana knew that it was not one building, but a complex comprising several palaces, courtyards, gardens, residences, and fortifications. Yet she could not have imagined the sheer size of it all.

Its dramatic location, situated on the edge of a rocky outcrop high above the city center, reminded Lana of its original military function. It really was the ideal place from which to defend Granada, Lana thought, as they rode increasingly higher up the hill. It was not until the mid-thirteenth century that the royal residence for the Nasrid Kingdom was built alongside the existing structures. Moorish kings continually expanded the complex until it was seized in 1492 by the Catholic monarchs. *Which explains the presence of the Charles V Palace*, Lana thought, which, according to her guidebook, was now regarded as an important example of Renaissance architecture in Spain.

As soon as they were out of the minivan, Lana and Randy rushed their group through the entrance, knowing they had a limited amount of time to get their guests to the first stop of the day—the Nasrid Palaces. It was the only section that required a timeslot reservation, due to its popularity and the tendency for visitors to spend an exorbitant amount of time taking in the spectacular architecture. The other two sections—the Alcazaba, or old military complex, and the Generalife gardens—also required an entrance ticket, but visitors could visit anytime throughout the day.

Getting around the Alhambra was a bit confusing due to its size and meandering layout. But once they oriented themselves, Lana and Randy speed-walked their group to the entrance of the Nasrid Palaces, the main palace and most popular section of the complex. They quickly passed through a seemingly empty courtyard, until Lana realized that the many stones sticking out of the ground were once the foundations of the homes of nobility, and the shops that once filled the immense space.

The signs for the palaces led to a regal Renaissance-style building whose presence momentarily confused Lana, until she realized, *This must be the Charles V Palace*. Having been forewarned that the attendants were quite strict about the timeslots, they rushed their group towards the entrance, despite their protests. After promising them they would have time to return after the Nasrid Palaces, the tour group hotfooted it through the fascinating oval building and courtyard to reach their destination on time.

When they entered the Nasrid Palaces complex, Lana gazed around in awe, speechless. Every surface—from the floor to the ceiling—was covered with elaborate patterns created from tiles, wood, plaster, and stone. Lana marveled at the intricateness of it all. *How long did it take to create this masterpiece?* she wondered while taking in the many carved surfaces and those embedded with colorful stones and mosaics. The brightly colored tiles contrasted wonderfully with the carved cream-colored wooden arches and ceilings rising high above them. The windows functioned as picture frames for the glorious vistas and stylized gardens that dotted the complex.

Lana knew it was listed as a UNESCO World Heritage site because it was a stunning example of Moorish architecture. Since figurative designs were forbidden by Islam, she figured the interiors would be rather dull. Nothing could have been further from the truth. The multitudes of shapes and textures played with the light and shadow. The walls seemed to shift as the sun's rays moved around the room, drawing Lana in as she kept watching for the next transformation. It was unlike anything she had ever seen and truly awesome.

Lana's neck ached from looking up so much. Not only were all of the walls and arches covered in extensive carvings and tile mosaics, but the ceilings were works of art all on their one. In the Hall of the Two Sisters, Lana wished she could lie down on the floor to better take in the enormous star covering the roof, carved so that it appeared to be expanding and twisting in the shifting light. In the Hall of the Abencerraje, stalactites made of carved wood seemed to drip down towards the visitors walking around underneath.

She meandered slowly through the extravagant spaces, glad her group wanted to walk around on their own. This was a site one could best experience alone, or at least without much distraction. Each door brought a new sensory experience. Lana didn't know which space she loved most—everywhere she looked, something beautiful caught her eye.

Even the courtyards were gorgeous. She had taken too many photos of the Courtyard of the Myrtles, attempting to capture the bright green color of the long pond in the center. Same went for the Palace of the Lions, so named because of the white stone statues of lions holding up a large fountain in the middle of the courtyard. Lana was convinced they would make the perfect shot for her blog post, but the images on her camera were not as spectacular as seeing the real thing. *Which is true for most amazing sights*, Lana realized. Nothing beat visiting a place in person.

When they regrouped an hour later, it was apparent that her group felt the same way. They talked over each other, all sharing what they enjoyed most about the decorations and spaces. Lana thought Dwight's absence would be the talk of the day, but so far, none of her guests seemed to notice or care.

When they reached the entrance to the Alcazaba, their group agreed to meet at a café close to the entrance in an hour, before they splintered off again. Lana resolved to get her interrogations over with, before she got swept up in the beauty of the place. Luckily for her, Ted and Serena both walked towards the stairs leading to the Vela Tower, the highest point within the Alcazaba complex.

After promising to check in with Randy as soon as she had finished grilling her guests, Lana went off to confront Ted and Serena. *If I make a point of staying close to other visitors, they won't be able to hurt me*, she told herself, trying to get her courage up. As much as she wanted Randy by her side, she figured his presence would make her clients clam up. He was, after all, a big guy. She, on the other hand, was more petite and female, which she hoped meant that neither of her guests would see her as a threat. The presence of many security guards milling about the palatial complex was a bonus, in Lana's book.

After their breathtaking visit to the Nasrid Palace, the Alcazaba was almost disappointing in comparison. Though the old military complex was not as decorative as the palatial residence they had just visited, the spectacular views made up for the lack of an interesting interior. It was perched right on the edge of the valley wall and overlooked all of Granada. The views of the city center and rolling Andalucían hills from the windows, balconies, and especially the Vela Tower were spectacular.

When she spotted Serena on top of the tower, she approached her cautiously, keeping well away from the roof's edge. She was slightly worried for her personal safety, until she realized the lifestyle blogger probably didn't wield anything sharper than a nail file.

Unfortunately, her conversation with the young woman did not go as she had hoped. After Lana reassured her that Dwight was off the tour for good, her attempts to get Serena to open up were met with dismissive disinterest.

"I wouldn't take anything Dwight said seriously. Everyone knows he is always trying to provoke people. I don't think he enjoys traveling, but he loves to criticize everyone who does."

When a large group of tourists entered the space, forcing all of those already on top of the tower to move aside to make room, Serena bounded away from her. As she watched the young woman scurry around the group and back down the stairs, Lana wondered if chasing after her would be a waste of time. Was Serena even capable of sticking a pin into Chet's throat? She did not seem like the violent type. So far, only Dwight fit that profile.

Figuring she wouldn't get anything more out of the blogger, Lana sought her next suspect. From her vantage point, she could see Ted and Erica down below in the maze-like Plaza de Armas. The square seemed to be a series of low walls and steps that led nowhere. *The sight would make Escher proud,* Lana thought. According to her guide, the ruins were the foundations of several homes, once occupied by servants working for the dignitaries and military personnel who also lived within the Alhambra complex.

Several gates blocked visitors from walking through the remains of the old homesteads. From up above, the space looked like a maze used by scientists to tests rats' intelligence. Lana hoped she could get in and out without having to ask for help.

As she walked briskly down the stairs and out to the courtyard, the incredible views momentarily pushed the angst she was feeling towards the back of her mind. Yet, as soon as she spotted Ted and Erica, a ball of anxiety formed in her stomach.

Lana strode over to her guest, determined to find out the truth about his argument with Dwight. There was no time to chitchat or beat around the bush—she needed answers if she was going to sleep soundly this evening. "Hey, Ted. Why did you promise to feature Dwight's work, but then back out?"

Erica clicked her tongue and stepped away from her fiancé, yet said nothing.

"What? No!" Ted laughed, but it sounded false and staccato. "I mean, we discussed the possibility. I thought it might be a good idea to give a new voice a chance, but it didn't work out, that's all."

Lana was so fed up with all of her clients' lies, her frustration finally boiled over. "Really? At the beginning of the tour, you were so convinced his work was not right for your website. Was he holding something over you, too? Does it have anything to do with Chet's room being broken into?"

"Of course not!"

"Then why did you change your mind and cancel Dwight's column after Chet was murdered?"

Ted frowned. "Chet's death had nothing to do with the timing. If you must know, a few potential investors grew concerned when they heard that Dwight would be working with us. Unfortunately, that young man's work is well known. His overly critical, elitist style is not appreciated by all. So I had to decide who was more important, Dwight or the sponsors. It was an easy decision to make, unfortunately for Dwight."

Lana nodded along. What he said made sense, but did not explain everything. *If only Dwight had told me the truth,* Lana thought. Now that she had kicked him off the tour, she could not speak with him easily. And there was no point in calling him. He had already blown her off in person and she doubted he would be more forthcoming on the phone.

When Ted held his arm out to Erica, Lana began to panic. Not ready to let him go, she tried another line of questioning. "Have you heard more from your lawyer about your website?"

Ted's face melted in relief. "Yes, he finally gave us the green light. He is convinced that I cannot be in competition with something that does not even exist. Now that Chet's site is in limbo, there's no way I can be stopped."

Lana cocked her head at him. "Interesting. Now that Chet is dead, there is no one left to invoke the noncompete clause or bad-mouth your site," she said as casually as she could while watching his reactions like a hawk.

"Yes—I, uh, guess you are right," Ted stammered.

"That's convenient," Lana began, hoping to move in for the kill, when Serena stepped into the courtyard. When she spotted Lana, the young blogger turned on her heel and exited as quickly as she'd entered.

"Oh, Serena, I need to talk with you about your feature," Ted called out as he sprinted to catch up to her. Lana and Erica were right on his heels.

Serena stopped and waited for Ted to catch up. "Sure. Do you want to grab a drink at the café by the Alcazaba's entrance? We should have a few minutes to chat before the rest join us."

"That would be great, thanks." He held out his arm to Erica. "Shall we?"

Erica shook her head slowly and pointed to a sign with a bathroom symbol on it. "You two go ahead. I'm going to find the restrooms, then I'll meet you there."

"Okay, kitten." Ted kissed his fiancée on the cheek before scurrying after Serena, who was already walking towards the café.

"It's been great chatting with you, Lana," Ted called out over his shoulder. "If you have any more questions about my website, you know where to find me."

Lana watched as he ran over to Serena and whispered something to her. Right before they rounded the corner, both looked nervously over their shoulders.

When the three made eye contact, Serena and Ted double-timed it out of her view. Something about how they were conspiring made Lana very nervous. She cast her thoughts back to the chaotic end to their flamenco workshop and Chet's murder, wondering whether she had missed something important. When she mentally reviewed the scene again, a new idea made her freeze. What if Dwight had not committed the crime, but knew who did?

He had been standing in between Ted and Serena when the lights went out. If one or both were involved in the murder, Dwight may have heard something that could incriminate them. Of her group, they did have the most to gain from Chet's demise.

As much as she wanted to call the detective in Seville and tell him about her suspicions, Lana couldn't point the finger at her clients without definitive proof. And she couldn't call Dotty, either. Her boss would most likely cancel the rest of the tour. Yet if she did, Lana and her group would still be suspects. Until she found solid proof of Serena and Ted's involvement, the tour had to go on.

38

Arm Strength

The more Lana thought about Serena and Ted working together, the more anxious she became. She called Randy, as promised, and they agreed to talk while their group was inside of the Generalife, the Alhambra's main gardens.

The two guides took up the rear, allowing them to see where their guests meandered off to as they spread out to explore the historical gardens. The Generalife once provided vegetables, fruits, and herbs for the residents of the Alhambra. It was also an oasis of relaxation, thanks to the many pools and fountains spurting water into the air. Gorgeous wildflowers, climbing vines, and flowering trees provided bursts of color and texture, contrasting nicely against the reddish walls. Everywhere she looked there were cedar, cypress, and palm trees towering high above, providing much-needed shade. Lana could imagine this would be the place to hang out and cool down during the hot summers.

As much as she was enjoying the views, Lana couldn't wait to tell Randy about her new suspicions. Yet, one niggling concern kept popping up in her mind—if Serena and Ted worked together to kill Chet, how did they devise the murder so quickly?

Lana couldn't recall them talking once during the workshop. Serena had danced with Amber and he with Erica. Besides, the murder could not have been premeditated—no one could have known that Lana would have a set of razor-sharp pins in her hair.

175

How she longed to talk with Alex about all of this. But she knew he was working, and even if she did reach him, it would take too long to catch him up. Instead, she sought the advice of his younger brother and her fellow guide.

"I think we might have sent the wrong person away," Lana whispered to Randy after pulling him to a corner bench and explaining her new theory. "If they had thrashed out a plan to harm Chet while standing in the hallway, Dwight would have heard them."

Randy's forehead creased. "Could they really have thought up such an evil plan in a matter of seconds? It seemed like the lights went out almost as soon as your group began walking into the hallway."

"I don't when they could have done so, otherwise. They weren't dancing together, and I don't recall seeing Ted check his phone. Though Dwight and Serena did several times. That's why I originally thought they may have been working together. But I don't think that anymore."

"Maybe we should cancel the tour. Or at least call the police inspector and let him know what is going on. It might help him solve this case," Randy reasoned.

"But we have no real proof—only my suspicions. And if we cancel the tour now, we will probably never know for certain if any of our guests murdered Chet."

"So what do we do now?" Randy asked.

"I say we continue on as planned. We only have two more days on the road before we head back to Seville. After that, we can't really keep tabs on them without it seeming suspicious. We did promise to keep the last three days free so they could watch the Semana Santa processions and celebrate Holy Week in their own way."

"I don't know if this is such a good idea, Lana. A lot can happen in two days. I don't think Serena or Ted could hurt me even if they tried, but I can't protect you the whole time."

"One of them probably pushed a pin through Chet's neck. That apparently didn't take much arm strength," Lana quipped.

"This isn't funny, Lana! If we do keep the tour going, then you have to promise to leave them alone. If you keep pestering them with questions, you will only be giving them a reason to hurt you, assuming one or both did harm Chet. We can keep our ears and eyes open, without confronting anyone."

"But will that get us our passports back? The inspector still hasn't gotten in touch with us. At least one of our guests is lying to us. I have already tried being nice and didn't get far," Lana countered. "If we don't provoke them, how are we going to figure out which one it is?"

"Assuming someone in our group murdered Chet," Randy stated. "Are you one hundred percent certain that Serena and Ted killed Chet? It might have been the Spanish dancer, Josepha. Chet said some pretty horrible things to her during the dance workshop. They must have known each other."

"I already talked to her, and I hate to say it, but I don't think she did it."

"What about Amber or the Sohos? Have you already looked into their backgrounds? Maybe they had a great reason to want to off him," Randy reasoned.

"I can almost guarantee you that Amber did not do it. She had never met Chet before and had absolutely no reason to murder him. And I did briefly suspect that the Sohos might have had a reason to harm him, but I am now certain they did not."

Randy's eyebrows shot up. "What made you change your mind and how can you be so sure?"

"Dwight made a few comments about an article he was writing about the Sohos and how their financial situation was less rosy than they let on. I thought that might have given them a reason to want Chet dead, but after reading his article, I realized I was wrong."

Before turning in last night, Lana had read through Dwight's rough draft. Despite his insinuations, her initial fear that her vlogging heroes had reason to murder Chet quickly dissipated. If anything, Dwight's short piece cleared the Sohos of the crime.

"And what did you discover?"

"That they have a lot of debt and aren't making enough with their blog to pay it all off. He predicted that they would be bankrupt by the end of the year, but Dwight must not have known that they had already signed the contract to present a television program when he wrote it. The money they will receive for presenting that show will surely be enough to cover their debts and keep them solvent."

"Okay, that makes sense," Randy said as he ran a hand through his wavy red hair. "Look, I know Dotty is pretty concerned about all the police investigations we seem to get embroiled with. Remember Paris? I was so certain we were going to lose you. I don't want to go through that again, especially now that you and my brother are a couple. He would never speak to me again if I let something bad happen to you. Why don't we sit this one out and just let the police do their work?"

Lana dropped her head so Randy couldn't see the anger flashing through her eyes. She knew he meant well, but she wasn't a delicate flower that needed protecting. On the other hand, she didn't want Randy to get so worried that he called their boss. The last thing she wanted to have happen was for Dotty to pull her off tour duty until her karma improved. Well, that and not be killed by whoever murdered Chet.

Two little things, Lana thought.

39

Bloodlust

April 14—Day Seven of the Wanderlust Tour in Ronda, Spain

Dinner was a blur, as was the late-night ride from Granada to Ronda. After they got everyone checked into their new hotel, Lana double-locked her door and placed a chair underneath the handle, just in case. She needed a good night's sleep if she was going to solve this mystery. Unfortunately her mind was not cooperating, and her thoughts kept racing through the night. The few moments of shut-eye she did get were filled with nightmares of being stabbed by hair accessories.

By the time she was dressed and downstairs for breakfast, her guests had finished their meals and were chatting about the upcoming day.

"Do we have time to visit the Plaza de Toros?" Ted asked Randy as Lana took a seat at their table.

"Yes, that should be possible. You have three hours to explore the city on your own before we meet up for lunch at that café close to the New Bridge," Randy said.

"You have got to be joking," Amber huffed. "I am not visiting a bullfighting ring, even if it is a museum."

"I thought you said it was important to put money in the hands of the locals," Ted said.

"Not if it glorifies the torture and killing of animals," she spat back.

"Bullfighting is part of Andalucía's rich cultural history! Heck, many consider Ronda to be the birthplace of the sport. Experiencing things like this is what real travel is all about," Ted countered. "That's where I'm heading first."

Lana shifted nervously in her seat. *Does Ted have a bloodlust?* She glanced at Serena, darting her eyes across the table in the hopes of avoiding direct eye contact. Lana didn't need to be so sneaky. The young blogger was so absorbed by whatever was on her telephone's tiny screen that she hadn't noticed Lana checking her out.

After her clients were sated, they split up for the day, promising to meet back at the hotel in time for lunch. Luckily, most of the city's many landmarks were within close proximity to each other, meaning there was no need to arrange transportation.

Their group spread out quickly. To Lana's dismay, Ted and Serena paired off, their heads close together as they whispered conspiratorially. Since Dwight had been kicked off the tour, those two had been spending quite a bit of time together. Amber and Erica trailed behind them. Becky and Nick waited until the others left, before heading off in the opposite direction.

Randy looked to Lana. "Want to walk with me?"

"Sure thing," she said with a smile, knowing he wanted to keep an eye on her, as much as he wanted her company.

They set off towards the historic city center, wanting to see the ancient Moorish palaces, many white houses, and colorful balconies Ronda was famous for, before visiting the main attraction—the El Tajo Canyon, a deep ravine that split the town in two.

After they'd walked a while in silence, Lana dared to ask Randy a question that she'd spent most of the night mulling over. "Why do people keep getting murdered during my tours?"

Randy frowned. "Technically, I was on all of the deadlier tours with you, so I guess it is our tours that attract killers. At least it wasn't one of our guests that was killed this time."

Lana stopped to let his words sink in. "Holy cow—you are right! It's not me, but us! And you're retiring, at least temporarily."

"Lana, why are you so happy all of a sudden?"

"Because I have been worried sick that Dotty is going to ground me because I'm some sort of killer-magnet. But you are right—we have been together when each of the murders happened. Since you are hanging up your tour guide's badge for the time being, maybe this streak of bad luck will be broken, as well. That way, Dotty doesn't have to clip my wings."

"That's one way of looking at it," Randy chuckled. "Is that why you didn't want me to talk with Dotty about all of this?"

Lana nodded, feeling guilty for not having told him the truth straight away.

"Tell you what, as long as no one else dies on this trip, I won't call Dotty." Randy stuck out his hand to shake on it.

The enormous grin on his face told her he was teasing. Yet, when she grasped his hand, Lana almost felt like she was tempting fate by agreeing.

40

Uninvited Guest

When Randy and Lana passed signs pointing to the New Bridge, they turned and followed. Not that they needed the official signs to know where to go. If the enormous hole in the earth was not a clue, the mass of tourists streaming in the same direction was.

They walked slowly along the path running parallel to the canyon until they reached the bridge deck. On either side were large groups huddled onto the narrow strips of sidewalk next to the edge, busy taking snapshots and videos of the dramatic scenery. Cars honked whenever tourists dared step onto the two-lane street to step around the others, meaning there was a cacophony of noise.

Lana and Randy were also the cause of several honking horns as they carefully maneuvered around the many groups. Neither wanted to be responsible for accidentally causing another to plummet to their deaths. The side railings, made of a stone that seemed to be crumbly in places, weren't that tall.

The bridge's popularity was justified—the views from it were astounding. From their high vantage point, Lana felt as if she could see all of southern Spain spread out before her feet. She glanced briefly down into the deep ravine and took in the river flowing through the massive blocks of stone, feeding a gaggle of plants and vines. Its dizzying depth made her stomach turn.

When they stopped to marvel at the homes and gardens built below the bridge and practically hanging over the cliffside, Lana spotted Amber, Erica, Ted, and Serena grouped together a few feet ahead. Luckily, they were so busy photographing the Andalucían countryside that they hadn't noticed either guide.

She began to steer Randy to the other side of the bridge and away from their guests when Amber's voice stopped them in their tracks.

"Dwight? What are you doing here?"

Amber's tense tone made both guides turn.

"No one can stop me from seeing the sights," Dwight said.

The menacing expression on his face made Lana's heart race. "Leave them alone, Dwight, or I'm calling the police," she yelled. He didn't seem to notice her threat and kept moving closer to the foursome.

A large group blocked the sidewalk and their path. Lana sprung into the road, causing a driver to swerve and honk as he cursed her out in Spanish. When she whipped around the group and jumped back onto the sidewalk, Randy was on her heels.

They had almost reached their guests when Dwight bore down on Ted, pushing the older man backwards towards the rather low stone railing lining the centuries-old bridge. "I am not leaving Spain empty-handed. You and Serena owe me!"

Erica stood frozen in place, her face a mask of terror and confusion. Serena and Amber both shrieked and darted away from Dwight.

"Don't you dare run away from me!" he screamed and grabbed at Serena, barely missing the blogger's shoulder.

When she whipped away from him and tore into the street, Dwight seemed momentarily torn as whether to follow her or not. Ultimately, he kept his sights set on Ted.

Dwight's face was a mask of rage. "If you don't feature my work, then I am going to the police. That will be the end of your precious website."

"I told you already, the deal is off. Chet is dead; you have nothing to hold over me anymore," Ted replied, puffing out his chest as he spoke.

"Why does everyone think they can steamroll over me? It's not fair!"

Dwight cried before rushing at Ted, his hands outstretched as if he intended to push the older man off the bridge.

Just before Dwight made contact, Ted threw himself face-first onto the sidewalk. Yet, Dwight's momentum kept propelling him forward. His leg caught on Ted's stomach, flinging him into the low railing too fast to stop himself from flying headfirst over the bridge.

The screams of many echoed through the deep valley as they witnessed Dwight's tragic fall. Tourists began running off the bridge in both directions, screaming for the police and an ambulance in a plethora of languages.

Erica fell into Ted's arms, weeping openly. A wave of nausea overtook Lana, sending her stumbling away from the rest as she crouched close to the bridge deck, afraid she might be sick. She closed her eyes and gulped back lungfuls of air until her stomach settled.

Randy followed her, concern etched on his face. "Are you alright?"

"That poor man. What a horrible way to die," she replied softly.

When she felt strong enough to stand, she and Randy crossed back over to their group.

"It was him or me," Ted stated, leaving no room for discussion. He continued stroking his fiancée's hair until her tears lessened.

"We know. We saw everything," Randy said. His reassurances seemed to put Ted at ease.

Lana eyed her guest warily, unsure what to believe. Was it truly a tragic coincidence, or had Ted somehow set Dwight up so that he would fall over?

Serena and Amber slowly walked back towards them, arm in arm, keeping their backs to the bridge's edge. Both were shaking visibly.

The senselessness of Dwight's death overwhelmed Lana. Whatever it was that he, Serena, and Ted were fighting about had caused this tragic accident, Lana realized as a wave of anger rose up inside of her.

"Why was Dwight so angry with you and Serena? He said he was going to go to the police. What was he holding over you two?" Lana implored.

"Who knows? He was clearly mentally unstable. He attacked me at the hotel and now this? I think I need to speak to a therapist," Serena said as she looked to Ted.

"Stop it! People are dying! Don't you get that?" Lana cried, tired of her guests' evasive games. "It is time for the truth to come out—before someone else dies."

When the pair looked to the ground, instead of making eye contact with Lana, she pressed again, "You two murdered Chet, didn't you? Did Dwight see you do it, or figure it out afterwards?"

"No!" both screamed simultaneously.

"Then come clean and tell me what is going on. Otherwise, I'm calling the detective." Lana already had her phone in her hand. She stepped back behind Randy so that they couldn't easily stop her from dialing. Randy, in turn, spread his shoulders out wide, making clear that Lana was not to be deterred.

"It wasn't the murder, but the break-in," Serena finally admitted. "That is what he was trying to use as blackmail."

Her answer made Lana freeze. "That was you? I was certain it was Ted."

Erica looked to the sky and shook her head slightly. Ted blushed as he cleared his throat. "Technically, I didn't ransack his room—Dwight did. But I did go inside."

"Why would you do that? What were you looking for?" Lana pressed.

"I needed to know when he was planning on launching his website. As long as mine was live first, he couldn't have touched me. But if he had launched his first, I would have had another legal battle to contend with."

"How the devil did you get in?" Lana asked.

"The door was already open," Ted said. He looked miserable. "Apparently Dwight left it open to scare Chet. He was waiting across the hallway for Chet to come back, which is how he got a picture of me entering the room. Dwight threatened to give it to the police if I didn't feature his work on my website. I wasn't inside Chet's room more than two minutes! And I didn't find anything useful, anyway."

"Oh, Ted," Erica moaned, her voice drenched in disappointment.

Lana frowned and folded her arms over her torso, unsure whether Ted was lying to her again. She turned to Serena. "How do you fit into all of this?"

"I gave Dwight the key and asked him to leave that creepy note on Chet's pillow."

Lana's fingers flew to her temples. "What? Okay, first of all, how did you get Chet's room key?"

"The night I tried talking him into accepting my settlement. After he refused to agree to my terms, I was so angry with him. When I left his room, his key card was next to the door, so I swiped it. I wasn't planning on doing anything with it, I just figured it would inconvenience him. But it did come in handy."

"So the break-in was a spur-of-the-moment thing for you, too? What were you searching for?"

"I wasn't looking for anything—heck, I didn't even go inside! I just wanted to scare Chet, that's all. When we heard he was out for the night, I persuaded Dwight to leave that note in exchange for a mention on my Instagram account. It didn't take a lot of convincing. Dwight had been moaning about what a jerk he thought Chet was; I simply exploited that. I would never break into someone's hotel room—my followers would never approve."

"Of course not. But they wouldn't mind that you sent Dwight in to do your dirty work?"

Serena averted her gaze.

"So what happened? Why did you two renege on your agreement with Dwight?"

Serena shrugged her shoulders. "After Chet died, I didn't see any reason to post about his magazine on my social media. The break-in was old news, and his work is so critical, it would have been a downer to talk about it. I didn't expect him to physically assault me if I didn't do what he asked."

Poor Dwight, Lana thought. No wonder he had felt as if everyone was taking advantage of him—they actually were.

"Okay, so now I understand why Dwight was trying to blackmail both of you into helping his writing career. But what does the break-in have to do with Chet's murder?" Lana asked.

"Nothing! I hated Chet and freely admit that I would have murdered him, if I'd had the chance. But I did not," Ted said. He looked so remorseful, it was difficult not to believe him.

"Me, either," Serena said, throwing her hand over her heart. "I may have suffered financially if Chet had won the lawsuit, but it was nothing that I couldn't bounce back from. My companies would still be worth millions."

Lana wondered whether Serena wasn't being a bit dramatic, but she got the point.

Sirens in the distance, approaching fast, made them all stop and turn towards the sound. A row of police cars, lights flashing, were racing through the small village.

"None of us killed Dwight. So what happens now?" Erica asked in a timid voice.

"The police are going to want to question all of us," Lana responded. How she wished this wasn't the first time she'd had to deal with such an incident. "Whatever you do, tell them the truth. You will regret it later, if you do not. Besides, there are so many tourists around here with cameras, someone is bound to have caught Dwight's death on film."

41

Whodunnit

Lana's head was spinning. *Two deaths in three days must be a new personal best,* she mused. Even worse, there was still a killer or two loose. She knew she should concentrate on what the police were asking her group, but she couldn't keep her mind focused on their current predicament.

The police were being meticulous in their questioning of everyone present on the bridge at the time of Dwight's death, which meant they were going to be here for quite a while. There were hundreds of tourists milling about when Dwight went over the edge. To ensure no one tried sneaking away, rows of uniformed officers sealed off both ends of the bridge deck.

A young officer had been assigned to their group, but his English was rather weak, lengthening the entire process. He had only questioned Serena so far, making a point of writing down her answers word for word in his tiny notebook. At this rate, they would not be on time for their lunch reservation, Lana realized. Not that it really mattered in light of all that had happened.

Being questioned by the Ronda police department made Lana's thoughts turn to their counterparts in Seville. *Wouldn't it be great if Chet's killer was not one of my group members this time,* she thought, hoping the detective was having more luck solving the case than she was.

Yet until he called to let her know that they could pick up their passports, she could not let up. *So who did it?* Lana asked herself. Several of her guests did have a motive, but all had reassured her that it was not a strong enough one to have risked a jail sentence for. *One of them must be a world-class liar,* she thought, though which one it was remained to be seen.

The young police officer finally wrapped up his questioning of Serena and had just turned to the Sohos, when Becky's phone rang. She smiled sheepishly at the officer and glanced at the screen. One look at the caller's name made her eyes shoot open. "Nick—it's Bob!" She sprung up and answered, moving quickly away from the group as she did. Nick trailed closely behind, moving so his ear was near the receiver.

"Come back here—I am not through questioning you!" the young officer demanded, but the Sohos kept moving farther away, seemingly oblivious to the policeman's pleas. When he began cursing in Spanish, Lana sprung up.

"I'll get them to come back," she reassured and sprinted after them.

The Sohos were standing a few feet away and huddled close together. As Lana moved closer, she realized they had put the call on speaker. A tinny voice was talking to them in a reassuring voice. "What are you worried about? Chet missed his chance. Forget about him, he's history. Literally, from what I hear. Is it true he was murdered during the travel expo?"

That must be their talent agent, Lana thought, the one they had been trying to reach for days. No wonder they had to take this call.

"That's true. But his obituary mentioned that the television show he was set to present was now in limbo. Is there anything you are not telling us?"

Their agent's laugh filled the speaker. "Chet's agent must have told the obituary writer that, and the paper didn't bother to fact-check it with the network. Chet is dead; the show is yours. Heck, it would be yours even if he was alive! I told you before, Chet got greedy. As long as you don't ask me to try to negotiate for more money..." The agent's voice trailed off, clearly waiting for the Sohos to answer his question.

"No! We still agree to all of the conditions," Nick exclaimed.

"Great! Then there is nothing to worry about."

To Lana's surprise, his words seemed to be draining the color from both Becky and Nick's faces. She stared at them, puzzled by their reaction. Their television show was never in jeopardy, so why were they upset?

"As soon as you fly in from Seville, we'll sign the contract, and then the network will make the official announcement that evening. So stop worrying and enjoy your trip. In fact, why don't you scout a few locations while you are there? We can suggest filming an episode of your new show in Andalucía. It is a popular destination, which is great for the ratings. I expect to see a shot list when you fly over."

Becky stammered, "Thanks for calling us back and reassuring us."

"Don't sweat it, kid. You aren't the first talent to get nervous. You two are going to be great. We'll see you in Los Angeles next week."

"We can't wait."

42

Jumping For Joy

Instead of jumping for joy, Becky and Nick looked as if they were about to burst into tears. Lana felt the same way. She had rightly guessed that two killers were involved, only she had been focusing her attention on the wrong pair. Because she had so much respect for Becky and Nick, she never seriously considered them as suspects in Chet's murder.

Dwight was right; I got sucked into their online presence. Despite their assurances to the contrary, they had not yet signed the contract for the television deal, meaning Chet had posed a real threat to their future.

"What have we done?" Becky muttered and buried her head in her hands.

Nick wrapped an arm around her shoulder. "We couldn't have known that he was lying to us."

"Did you kill Chet for the money?" Lana whispered.

The Sohos looked to Lana, a stricken expression on their faces.

"It's not that simple," Becky pleaded.

"I think it is. Dwight had been investigating your finances for a new article and discovered that you are deep in debt. You needed the television deal to survive financially, didn't you? And Chet could have ruined it all—or so you thought."

Becky hung her head low. "We have worked so hard for so many years, but we still haven't earned enough to pay off all of our debts. Without this deal, we would have had to get nine-to-five jobs again. We couldn't go back, not after ten years of freedom."

"Let me guess. When you found out he was also attending the flamenco workshop, you devised a plan to kill him."

Lana glanced at Nick but he couldn't look her in the eyes. Becky's mouth formed a tiny O as she shook her head emphatically. The way her short bob danced around her face, brought another flash of realization to the forefront of Lana's mind.

"Of course! I was so sure the murder could not have been premeditated because no one would have known that the hair combs were attached to razor-sharp pins. But you knew there would be a murder weapon present, didn't you, Becky?"

When Becky began shaking her head again, Lana added, "The *peinetas* you wore in your hair during that two-day flamenco workshop in Argentina was beautiful. I watched the video after you mentioned it to our instructor. It's too bad you cut your hair off before this trip—otherwise you could have used your hair comb to kill Chet, instead of mine!"

Becky's shoulders caved in. "It wasn't supposed to work out like this."

Nick suddenly leapt to his feet and pushed his way through the crowd. When Lana raced after him, Becky sprung up and ran off in the opposite direction.

"Help, police! You have to stop them! They killed Chet Rogers!" Lana screamed as hard as she could while pointing at the Sohos.

Several officers responded, chasing after the couple as best they could. But there were so many groups hanging around the bridge, waiting to be questioned, that they had to dodge hundreds of tourists in their pursuit.

A feisty-looking granny used her walking stick to take down Becky, but Nick managed to sprint away from the crowd, leaving a group of panting officers in his wake. When he approached the line of policemen blocking the end of the bridge deck, Nick launched himself off the low wall and into a garden hanging precariously close to the cliff's edge, before he jumped their fence and raced off again.

"He's getting away!" Lana cried, until she noticed several policemen speaking rapidly into their walkie-talkies. She doubted Nick would get far.

Two policemen had Becky in handcuffs. They sat her down on the pavement before other policemen cleared the bridge, presumably to make way for a police car.

Lana sat down next to her vlogging hero, wondering where it all had all gone wrong for the Sohos.

"Did you stab Chet, or did Nick?"

Becky stared straight ahead and stayed silent for so long, Lana thought she hadn't heard her. *Maybe it was the shock of getting caught*, Lana thought as she began to rise.

"Nick's so tall, we figured someone would notice him moving around, even in the dark. That's why I dropped my hair clip, so I would have an excuse to go back and look for it. And then you conveniently bent over to loosen your shoe's buckle at precisely the right moment, which made it even easier for me to grab the comb. Sorry for pulling so hard on your hair," Becky said.

The sincerity of her apology broke something inside of Lana. "Why did Chet have to die?"

"It was his own fault. He lied about being able to hinder our deal. We had made a few jokes about stabbing him with a *peinetas* during the workshop, but we never would have acted on it if he hadn't taunted us like that. We sacrificed everything to get as far as we have, and we were not going to let Chet destroy it all."

Becky blew out her cheeks and sighed. "We should have called our agent straightaway. It would have saved us a world of hurt."

"And Chet's life," Lana replied softly.

43

Crazy Money

After Lana watched Becky being placed into the back of the police car, she buried her head in her hands and wept. It was the senselessness of it all that drove Lana to despair. Why did money make people so crazy? As much as she disliked Chet, she couldn't condone his murder—especially for something so meaningless.

After she had pulled herself together, Lana found Randy sitting on the edge of the sidewalk with the remains of their tour group. "I'm going to go to the police station and camp out in their lobby until Becky admits she and Nick killed Chet. Once she does, the rest of us should be free from suspicion."

Randy nodded in acknowledgement. "Sounds good. I'll get the rest back to the hotel." His face was paler than usual, and his eyes seemed unfocused. Lana could imagine that he too was dazed by the Sohos' actions.

Lana walked over to the police station, hoping the fresh air would help clear her head. When she approached the building, Nick was being taken out of a police car in handcuffs. *That didn't take long*, she thought, happy to see that he had not gotten away. From what the Ronda police were willing to share with her, Becky had immediately confessed to the crime, framing her and Nick's actions as if they murdered Chet in self-defense.

After conferring with his counterpart in Seville, the local police inspector announced that Lana and the rest of her group were no longer suspects in the murder investigation and could pick up their passports as soon as they were back in Seville.

When she returned to the hotel, her elation turned to irritation. The parking lot was filled with trucks and buses bearing the names and logos of television stations from around the world. *How did they get here so quickly?* she wondered.

Lana had called Randy before leaving the police bureau and knew their group would be waiting for her in the hotel's restaurant. Because their day in Ronda was cut short by Dwight's death and the Sohos' arrest, Lana wasn't certain what the mood would be. To her surprise, the rest of the group were more interested in sharing their version of events with the media than the fates of their fellow tourists.

She took a seat at their table, ordering a salad that she knew she would not eat, and leaned back in her chair. When her phone rang and she saw that it was her friend Jeremy, Lana sent the call to voicemail and turned off her ringer. There would be time enough to talk to the media later.

Randy popped over and sat down next to her. "How are you feeling?"

"Exhausted. And sorry—for you, anyway. This is your last tour, at least for the time being. It's not exactly the ideal sendoff."

"It would have been nice if the week had remained fatality-free, but there wasn't much we could do about that," Randy agreed.

"I'm glad you think so. Let's hope Dotty shares your opinion."

"I already talked with her and caught her up on the arrests."

Lana tensed up. "Did she say anything about grounding me for a while?"

Randy shook his head. "She didn't say a word about it. Why don't you take the rest of the day off? You look like you could fall asleep at any moment."

"You're right about that. I can barely keep my eyes open. Now that Chet's killers are in custody, I might actually be able to sleep through the night." Lana rose and gave her friend a quick hug. "Thanks for being there for me, Randy. I am really going to miss working with you."

Randy chuckled. "Who says I won't guide another tour one day? And anyway, as long as you and Alex are together, we'll see enough of each other at family barbeques and birthdays."

Lana's eyes widened. "What do you mean, as long as?"

"Lana! You're reading too much into my words. Go take a nap. Or better yet, call your boyfriend. His conference should have ended an hour ago. I bet he'll be able to talk now."

Lana saluted. "Yes, sir!" She pecked her fellow guide on the cheek and skipped towards the elevator, hoping Alex did, indeed, have time for her.

44

Second Chances

April 17—Day Ten of the Wanderlust Tour in Seville, Spain

The streets before her were filled with thousands of robed and hooded figures, walking slowly behind swaying life-sized religious effigies, many decorated with gigantic palm fronds. Blaring horns, jingling bells, and pounding drums accompanied the ritualistic procession. Incense wafted across the parade and onlookers, creating a sweetly scented mist that added to the mystical atmosphere. Spectators threw flower petals and confetti at the passing statues and floats, so much so that it seemed to be snowing at times.

Semana Santa was unlike anything Lana had ever witnessed. The pageantry, ceremonies, costumes, music, and rituals were incredibly fascinating, and she felt so lucky to see this heavenly spectacle in person.

More than fifty Brotherhoods—or religious fraternities—took part in this ancient celebration of Christ's death and resurrection. Each Brotherhood had its own Virgin Mary and Jesus statues, as well as colorful artwork illustrating parts of the Easter story, some dating as far back as the seventeenth century. These ancient religious objects were displayed on elaborately decorated floats that were carried by bearers hidden underneath. Each day, several Brotherhoods provided an extravagant procession of musicians, floats, and penitents as they walked from their parish churches to the Seville Cathedral, and then back again. Some of the larger groups took up to fourteen hours to make the round trip.

On the street before her, cries and cheers announced the arrival of a massive throne covered in gold. A realistically painted Virgin Mary stood upon it, waving a hand over the crowd as if she was blessing them. Her intricately embroidered mantle trailed far behind her.

Following the religious statues were hundreds, and in some cases thousands, of *nazarenos* or penitents carrying bowls of burning incense, candles, or crosses. Their body-covering robes and tall, pointed hoods that hid their faces were simultaneously beautiful and unsettling. Their garb, originating from the sixteenth century, was designed so the faithful could repent in anonymity. Yet their pointy hoods did bear a strong resemblance to those later used by the Ku Klux Klan. Lana had to remind herself that this religious tradition existed long before the United States did.

It seemed as if all of Seville was out celebrating Easter Sunday and the last day of the Holy Week. Since returning from Ronda, she and her group had been consumed by the festivities. It was her third day of watching the processions, but she was still mesmerized by the entire experience. The combination of costumes, rituals, incense, and music was magical.

From her position on a balcony overlooking the official procession route, Lana could see the entire street, filled with hundreds—if not thousands—of onlookers crammed onto the narrow sidewalks. Simply seeing them all squished together made her claustrophobic.

Lana was grateful that Dotty had booked them into a hotel along the official route, so they had the option of watching the parade from their rooms' balconies. Not only did they have an unobstructed view of the official route, but they also had a restroom at their disposal. It was perfect.

Randy and most of her tour group were down there somewhere, in amongst the masses. After being sandwiched into one place all morning, Lana decided to enjoy the afternoon's events from above. Because she was too short to see over most of the other onlookers, the view from here was actually better.

The incredible sights and sounds also helped clear her mind. After discovering Becky and Nick had killed Chet, Lana had been overcome by a deep-seated sadness that she'd had trouble shaking.

It was only after talking to her boyfriend, Alex, that Lana finally realized how stressed out she had been these past few weeks. It wasn't just the extra work or deaths on several of her tours that was doing her head in. The mental and emotional strain of Alex being distant, her not being there for Willow, and Randy leaving his job as guide were all taking a toll on her.

After spending an afternoon catching up with her boyfriend, she realized that she was a fool to think he was falling out of love with her. She had doubted his fidelity because he was unable to respond to her messages immediately, yet she now knew firsthand how stressful the conferences he worked at could be. His many reassurances of his love and commitment to her put her mind and heart at ease. And his idea to meet up in Venice after her next tour ended only confirmed his sincerity.

Once their group was back in Seville, she had gotten in touch with Willow. Lana did so with hesitation, uncertain how she would respond to her call. Lana's heart went out to her best friend, who was so tired that she was yawning for most of their conversation. Yet Willow still cracked jokes, sharing anecdotes about her life as a mother with her childless friend. Lana laughed along, glad Willow could see the lighter side of her sometimes-frustrating new role. Lana's promise to babysit the next time she was back in Seattle brought a spark of joy to her otherwise exhausted friend's eyes. And Willow's protests that she wanted to have a girls' night out first was music to Lana's ears.

For the first time in several weeks, Lana felt positive about her relationship with both Willow and Alex.

Yet when her phone rang, the number on the screen made her stomach clench. She had one more crisis to deal with. Knowing she could not avoid Dotty any longer, Lana took a deep breath and answered as jovially as she could.

"Lana Hansen, what are we going to do with you?" her boss sighed into the phone. "It's only April and your body count is at three. It is getting spooky how many people die during your tours. Maybe you should stop leading them for a while."

"I am not a magnet for murderers," Lana said resolutely as she put a finger in her free ear, in a futile attempt to dim the noise of the crowd. "It's more of a streak of bad luck. And now that Randy is retiring, I hope that my luck is about to change."

"Randy told me about your theory. He sure is rooting for you."

"Yes, he is. Look, it's too late to ground me, anyway. I am flying to Venice tomorrow to get everything ready for my next tour. I say we see what happens before discussing whether to take me off guide duty. If no one dies during that one, we will know that this curse has been broken."

Dotty was silent for quite a long time, presumably mulling Lana's idea over. "It's a deal," she finally responded, to Lana's enormous relief. "I really don't want to clip your wings because I know how much you enjoy the work."

Lana jumped around in joy, glad her boss was so receptive to her suggestion. "Thank you, Dotty! I sure hope this works."

"Me, too. But we have to do something and your reasoning sounds as good as any. I guess we will have to have faith that it will work out this time," Dotty reasoned.

"Faith?" Lana repeated. That wasn't the word that sprung to mind, but perhaps it was the correct one, she thought as she looked out over the crowd of devout worshippers. The extraordinary sight before her was the ultimate expression of faith, trust, and belief in a higher power.

"I can do that," Lana said, her voice strong. Instead of worrying about things she couldn't control, she had to focus on those that she could. And with Dotty, Alex, and Willow on her side, she could get through anything.

THE END

Thanks for reading *Death by Flamenco*!

Reviews really do help readers decide whether they want to take a chance on a new author. If you enjoyed this story, please consider posting a review on BookBub, on Goodreads, or with your favorite retailer. I appreciate it!
Jennifer S. Alderson

Follow the further adventures of Lana Hansen in *Death by Gondola: A Springtime Murder in Venice*.

Venice—the city of canals, masks...and murder?

Tour guide Lana Hansen's trip to Venice is brought to an abrupt halt when her boyfriend is arrested for murdering the owner of a cruise ship. Can she sleuth out the real killer before her partner's visit to the Floating City becomes permanent?

Available as paperback and eBook in April 2022. Preorder it now on Amazon!

Acknowledgments

I want to thank my wonderful family for helping me create the time and space to write during the many lockdowns and school closures.

My editor, Sadye Scott-Hainchek of The Fussy Librarian, continues to do an excellent job polishing this series, and I am grateful for her outstanding work and advice. The cover designer for this series, Elizabeth Mackey, constantly amazes me with her gorgeous and fun designs.

I hope this book and the others in my Travel Can Be Murder series help to sate your wanderlust during these trying times. Stay safe, dear readers.

About the Author

Jennifer S. Alderson was born in San Francisco, raised in Seattle, and currently lives in Amsterdam. After traveling extensively around Asia, Oceania, and Central America, she moved to Darwin, Australia, before finally settling in the Netherlands. Her background in journalism, multimedia development, and art history enriches her novels. When not writing, she can be found in a museum, biking around Amsterdam, or enjoying a coffee along the canal while planning her next research trip.

Jennifer's love of travel, art, and culture inspires her award-winning Zelda Richardson Mystery series, her Travel Can Be Murder Cozy Mysteries, and her standalone stories.

Book One of the Zelda Richardson Mystery series—*The Lover's Portrait*—is a suspenseful whodunit about Nazi-looted artwork that transports readers to WWII and present-day Amsterdam. Art, religion, and anthropology collide in *Rituals of the Dead* (Book Two), a thrilling artifact mystery set in Papua and the Netherlands. Her pulse-pounding adventure set in the Netherlands, Croatia, Italy, and Turkey—*Marked for Revenge* (Book Three)—is a story about stolen art, the mafia, and a father's vengeance. Book Four—*The Vermeer Deception*—is a WWII art mystery set in Germany and the Netherlands.

The Travel Can Be Murder Cozy Mysteries follow the adventures of tour guide and amateur sleuth Lana Hansen. Book One—*Death on the Danube*—takes Lana to Budapest for a New Year's trip. In *Death by Baguette* (Book Two), Lana escorts five couples on an unforgettable Valentine-themed vacation to Paris. In Book Three—*Death by Windmill*—Lana's estranged mother joins her Mother's Day tour to the Netherlands. In Book Four—*Death by Bagpipes*—Lana accompanies a famous magician and his family to Edinburgh during the Fringe Festival. In Book Five—*Death by Fountain*—Lana has to sleuth out who really killed Randy Wright's ex-girlfriend, before his visit to Rome becomes permanent. In Book Six, *Death by Leprechaun*, needs the luck of the Irish to clear her friend of a crime. In Book Seven—*Death by Flamenco*— Lana has to sleuth out a murderer if she is to dance her way out of a jail sentence. Book Eight, *Death by Gondola*, will be released in April 2022.

Jennifer is also the author of two thrilling adventure novels: *Down and Out in Kathmandu* and *Holiday Gone Wrong*. Her travelogue, *Notes of a Naive Traveler*, is a must-read for those interested in traveling to Nepal and Thailand. All three are available in the *Adventures in Backpacking* box set.

For more information about the author and her upcoming novels, please visit Jennifer's website or sign up for her newsletter.

Death on the Danube: A New Year's Murder in Budapest

Book One of the Travel Can Be Murder Cozy Mystery Series

Who knew a New Year's trip to Budapest could be so deadly? The tour must go on—even with a killer in their midst...

Recent divorcee Lana Hansen needs a break. Her luck has run sour for going on a decade, ever since she got fired from her favorite job as an investigative reporter. When her fresh start in Seattle doesn't work out as planned, Lana ends up unemployed and penniless on Christmas Eve.

Dotty Thompson, her landlord and the owner of Wanderlust Tours, is also in a tight spot after one of her tour guides ends up in the hospital, leaving her a guide short on Christmas Day.

When Dotty offers her a job leading the tour group through Budapest, Hungary, Lana jumps at the chance. It's the perfect way to ring in the new year and pay her rent!

What starts off as the adventure of a lifetime quickly turns into a nightmare when Carl, her fellow tour guide, is found floating in the Danube River. Was it murder or accidental death? Suspects abound when Lana discovers almost everyone on the tour had a bone to pick with Carl.

But Dotty insists the tour must go on, so Lana finds herself trapped with nine murder suspects. When another guest turns up dead, Lana has to figure out who the killer is before she too ends up floating in the Danube...

Available as paperback, large print edition, eBook, and in Kindle Unlimited.

Death on the Danube
Chapter One: A Trip to Budapest

December 26—Seattle, Washington

"You want me to go where, Dotty? And do what?" Lana Hansen had trouble keeping the incredulity out of her voice. She was thrilled, as always, by her landlord's unwavering support and encouragement. But now Lana was beginning to wonder whether Dotty Thompson was becoming mentally unhinged.

"To escort a tour group in Budapest, Hungary. It'll be easy enough for a woman of your many talents."

Lana snorted with laughter. *Ha! What talents?* she thought. Her resume was indeed long: disgraced investigative journalist, injured magician's assistant, former kayaking guide, and now part-time yoga instructor—emphasis on "part-time."

"You'll get to celebrate New Year's while earning a paycheck and enjoying a free trip abroad, to boot. You've been moaning for months about wanting a fresh start. Well, this is as fresh as it gets!" Dotty exclaimed, causing her Christmas-bell earrings to jangle. She was wrapped up in a rainbow-colored bathrobe, a hairnet covering the curlers she set every morning. They were standing inside her living room, Lana still wearing her woolen navy jacket and rain boots. Behind Dotty's ample frame, Lana could see the many decorations and streamers she'd helped to hang up for the Christmas bash last night. Lana was certain that if Dotty's dogs hadn't woken her up, her landlord would have slept the day away.

"Working as one of your tour guides wasn't exactly what I had in mind, Dotty."

"I wouldn't ask you if I had any other choice." Dotty's tone switched from flippant to pleading. "Yesterday one of the guides and two guests crashed into each other while skibobbing outside of Prague, and all are hospitalized. Thank goodness none are in critical condition. But the rest of the group is leaving for Budapest in the morning, and Carl can't do it on his own. He's just not client-friendly enough to pull it off. And I need those five-star reviews, Lana."

Dotty was not only a property manager, she was also the owner of several successful small businesses. Lana knew Wanderlust Tours was Dotty's favorite and that she would do anything to ensure its continued success. Lana also knew that the tour company was suffering from the increased competition from online booking sites and was having trouble building its audience and generating traffic to its social media accounts. But asking Lana to fill in as a guide seemed desperate, even for Dotty, and even if it was the day after Christmas. Lana shook her head slowly. "I don't know. I'm not qualified to—"

Dotty grabbed one of Lana's hands and squeezed. "Qualified, shmalified. I didn't have any tour guide credentials when I started this company fifteen years ago, and that hasn't made a bit of difference. You enjoy leading those kayaking tours, right? This is the same thing, but for a while longer."

The older lady glanced down at the plastic cards in her other hand, shaking her head. "Besides, you know I love you like a daughter, but I can't accept these gift cards in lieu of rent. If you do this for me, you don't have to pay me back for the past two months' rent. I am offering you the chance of a lifetime. What have you got to lose?"

* * *

Are you enjoying the book so far? Why not buy *Death on the Danube* now and keep reading!

Available as paperback, large print edition, eBook, and in Kindle Unlimited.

www.ingramcontent.com/pod-product-compliance
Lightning Source LLC
Chambersburg PA
CBHW071246150726
48001CB00018B/217